Kittery Ghost

by

Barbara T. Winslow

North
Country
Press

Kittery Ghost

Cover art by Tammi Galbraith

Copyright © 2016 by Barbara T. Winslow

ISBN 978-1-943424-09-2
Library of Congress Control Number: 2016938947

North Country Press
Unity, Maine

For my grandchildren...Rory, Cadi, Colt, Emi and Winn...may all the ghosts in your lives be friendly.

Haunted House

Rain and wind alternately pelted the bubbled window panes on the second floor of the old Wentworth house, where Tom Pendly lay rigid beneath his quilts. He held his breath, but the only sound he heard was wind whistling through the cracks in the ancient clapboards and under weathered shingles.

From the room down the hall, Tom heard the bed springs creak as his seven-year-old stepsister, Anna, turned restlessly in her sleep. Young as she was, Tom felt some comfort in her presence here tonight. For Tom felt sure that somewhere in this house, tonight, there was another presence.

"Bong, bong," the grandfather clock in the hallway began the soft, muffled chiming of the hour. Tom lay still and counted. "Nine, ten, eleven, twelve..." SLAM! Tom jolted upright as the door in the front hallway slammed.

He stared into the empty blackness of his room, scarcely breathing. The wind outside kept up its steady whine but inside there was a deep stillness.

If only his parents would get home. They hadn't planned to be out this late. He had sometimes been left alone or with a "sitter," especially before his mother had married Paul Chenard. She had worked late at her law office, or she had brought her work home and Tom had fallen asleep to the steady scratching of her pen. But that was before she had met Paul and they had moved to Kittery, Maine. Now Tom's life was completely different.

After Tom's father had died while in the Air Force, his mother had vowed she would make a good life for herself and Tom. So for eleven years Tom and his mother had lived alone and that's how Tom thought it was always going to be. Then she met Paul, and here they were.

It was very easy to blame Paul for his present discomfort. Tom had never lived in an old house before. This wasn't just old, it was historical. But Tom wasn't really interested in its history. He just knew it was old and drafty and in need of lots of work. That's why Paul, who was a carpenter, had bought it. He fixed up old homes for a living, and boats for the love of it.

So maybe it was also haunted, thought Tom now, as he tossed in his bed. He knew the front and back doors were locked and all the windows were locked too. He also knew that the Kittery police regularly patrolled past this section of town.

"Anyway, there isn't any such thing as ghosts," Tom reasoned as he lay back against the soft pillow and pulled the quilts up to his chin. Moments later, Tom heard the front door open and close. He held his breath listening for familiar footsteps. They must have gone into the living room, he thought sleepily to himself. Well, it was about time they were home. Feeling the comfort of their presence, Tom at last drifted into a deep sleep. He didn't hear the car pull into the driveway an hour later when his parents returned from their night out.

Invader

Sunlight flickered across Tom's face and a warm sea breeze brushed his curtains back when next he opened his eyes. The spooky feeling from the night before was completely forgotten as he wiggled out of bed and padded over to the window. Stretching in the morning sun, Tom looked appreciatively towards the harbor. If there was one reason he was glad they had moved to Kittery, it was having the Atlantic Ocean practically at his doorstep. He watched the white sails bob and sway, trying to pick out his stepfather's sleek new sailboat before dressing quickly and running down to breakfast.

Paul was in the kitchen finishing his standard breakfast of bacon and eggs. Anna was sitting near him but she wasn't eating. Tom glanced at her briefly before heading for the cereal bowls.

"Mornin', Tom," said Paul. "If you'd a slept any longer, you'd of had the whole house to yourself."

"If *you'd* come home earlier," Tom answered sarcastically," I might have been able to get some sleep." He knew he sounded bad tempered so he smiled at his stepfather as he spoke. Paul looked at him in surprise.

"But, Tom, you were sound asleep when we got home last night. I know it was late...late for me too. I'm not used to these late nights. Sorry if we worried you, son, but there won't be many one o'clock evenings for us."

Tom liked it when Paul called him "son." He instantly forgave him for the worrisome night.

"You weren't even that late, Paul. It was only midnight. The clock had just finished chiming when you came in."

"Well, you must have drifted off to sleep again, 'cause it was just one o'clock when we pulled in the yard."

Tom stood still in the center of the kitchen floor. He wouldn't argue with Paul, but he knew he had heard the door open and close at midnight. If it hadn't been Paul and his mother, who was it? Slowly Tom reached for the bowl and set it on the table. "Maybe it was a dream," he said. "I must have been confused." But even as he said that, he remembered the sound of the door opening and closing. Still, it wasn't worth starting a fight.

While he ate his cereal, Anna sat quietly and watched him. Tom scowled at her until she turned away. "Pest," he thought to himself. Paul put his dishes in the sink and called to Anna. "Come on, little one, let's get to the shipyard and get to work on that boat." He helped Anna zip her jacket. Tom watched them without speaking.

"Your mom is working, Tom, and she'll be at the office until about two o'clock. She said to make your own lunch. Leave a note if you go out, O.K.?" Paul took Anna's hand and went out the kitchen door.

"O.K.," Tom nodded as the door closed. "As if you'd care," he mumbled under his breath. He would have liked to go to the shipyard too. Anyway, it would have been nice to be asked.

When Anna stayed for the weekend, Paul took her everywhere. When she wasn't with them, Paul would ask Tom along. "It isn't fair," he thought to himself. Tom thought about the day ahead of him. He was new at school and didn't know many kids yet. But sometimes he'd run into some of his classmates down at the harbor. It was a good place to see what was going on.

Suddenly, Tom felt a chill pass over him. He shivered and stood up to put his dishes in the sink. The house seemed strangely quiet and empty. "I guess I'll head down towards the harbor," he announced to the empty house. His voice echoed eerily around him. Without leaving a note, Tom stepped out the door and closed it firmly behind him. Crossing the road towards the library, Tom looked back over his shoulder at the large colonial house which was now his home. It seemed solid and substantial, guarding the corner of the road leading from the town out to the country.

Tom shrugged his shoulders to throw off the uneasy feeling he'd had moments before. Just as he was turning away, he saw a movement in the living room window. As Tom watched closely, the curtains were parted and an old man stood staring right into Tom's eyes.

A Spooky Visitor

For one chilling moment, Tom stood rooted to his spot. Wheeling around, he ran up the granite steps to the public library which was behind him. "Someone must have gotten into the house last night," Tom thought as he stumbled up the steps. Yanking open the heavy oak door he turned immediately to the office. His heart raced and his breath came in gasps as he grabbed the phone.

"Mrs. Borden, I need to use the phone," he explained as he dialed his mother's number. "Somebody's in our house!" The librarian rose quickly and went to the window. She said calmly, "Why Tom, I just saw your father leave a moment ago. Are you sure there's somebody in there? Don't you want to call the police?" By that time Tom heard his mother answering the phone. "Pendly and Carpenter Law Offices."

"Mom, I just left the house and Paul and Anna are gone too. But when I looked back, I saw an old man in the window." Tom's voice shook.

"Where are you, Tommy?"

"I'm at the library, Mom. Do you want me to go get Paul?"

"No, Tom. You stay put. I'll call Paul. He's at the boatyard and I'll have him go right home. Now don't leave the library."

Tom was shaking as he hung up the phone. He and Mrs. Borden stood at the window watching the house. Nothing moved in the window. After some minutes Tom grew restless and Mrs. Borden sat back down at her desk to finish her work. Tom paced the room nervously until Mrs. Borden smiled up at him. "Why don't you go wait on the front steps, Tom. When your father gets home, you'll see him right away."

"Thanks, Mrs. Borden, I'll do that." Tom walked out the door and sat facing his house. Nothing moved. No sound came from his home. After a moment he got up and walked down the steps. Watching the window closely, Tom ran quickly across the road. He began to feel foolish. Suppose he had just imagined that he had seen an old man.

Silently, Tom ran up to the side of the house. "If I can just peek in the window, I might see him again," he reasoned. Hugging the old house, Tom inched his way around to the kitchen window. Wiping his sweaty hands on his jeans, Tom reached up to the window sill and taking a deep breath he peered cautiously into the kitchen.

"Yikes!" Tom screamed and fell back to earth with a bang. The steely blue eyes and white bearded face of the stranger looked right at Tom.

"Geeze," Tom breathed as he pushed himself tightly against the side of the house. He wanted to run but his watery legs wouldn't hold him. His breath came in ragged gasps. His one thought was escape. Pushing himself onto his knees, Tom began to crawl frantically back towards the road when he felt something tug on his pants. Tom screamed and kicked. "Let go!" But whatever was holding his pants hung on.

Jerking his legs this way and that, he yelled again, "Let go, please!!"

"Leave him be, Pompey," ordered a deep voice. Tom looked excitedly around to see who was rescuing him. But nobody was there. However, the pants were instantly released and Tom scrambled to his feet.

"Wh..who's there?" he asked, backing against the house. In front of him the leaves suddenly blew in a tiny whirlwind...then settled back peacefully at Tom's feet. Just as surely as there had been someone there moments before, now Tom knew he was alone.

At that very moment Paul walked around the side of the house with Anna at his heels.

"Are you all right?" he asked quickly, grabbing hold of Tom.

"Ye..yes...I guess so. Man, am I ever glad to see you!"

Paul studied Tom's white face and shaking body for a moment.

"Is someone in the house, Tom?"

"No...not now, not anymore, that is." Tom thought of how he could explain all this. But Paul didn't give him a chance. He strode purposefully into the house telling Anna to "stay put."

Tom heard Paul walking through the house, opening and slamming doors. Anna stood near Tom but didn't say anything. Tom, still shivering, sat down under the oak tree and took deep breaths. He was still there moments later when his mother pulled into the driveway and rushed into the house. Tom heard her talking to Paul. Then the door banged as she hurried into the yard and over to Tom.

"Are you all right, Tom? Are you hurt? Oh why did you come back over here?" She put her arms around him and held him for a moment.

Usually Tom didn't let his mother get away with this kind of "hands on" affection. But right now he welcomed her nearness. He breathed deeply of the lilac scent she used and closed his eyes. Under her soothing hands, he finally stopped shaking.

"Now tell me everything that happened," she said. Tom drew a ragged breath and began at the beginning, which was really the night before when he had heard someone come into the house at midnight. Paul had joined them and he listened closely as Tom told about seeing the old man in the window and then something holding onto his pant leg. And when he told about hearing somebody talk, when nobody was there, Paul and his mother exchanged worried glances.

"Ellen," Paul said, "I think we better have a talk before we do anything. I've been all through the house, and nothing has been disturbed that I can see. You come check to see if there's anything missing and then we'll see about calling the police."

Tom watched as his mother and Paul walked into the house. "They don't believe me," he thought to himself. "They think I'm crazy."

Anna was still sitting near him and Tom looked over at her expecting some wise remark. But instead she put her hand on his sleeve and asked, "Do you think it was a ghost, Tom?"

"I don't know what I think. All I know is what happened and I don't understand any of it." Anna nodded and looked up at the house. "I hope it's a ghost," she said. "I always wanted to meet a real ghost."

Tom shrugged his shoulders and said sarcastically, "If you want to meet a ghost, I hope you keep it to yourself."

Tom's mother had heard his last remark as she walked out to sit beside him under the oak. She took his hand and smiled at both of them.

"Well, Tom, you know I don't believe there was any ghost here. There has to be a logical explanation for everything. Either there was really someone in the house, or your mind is playing tricks on you for some reason. I know you didn't make up this story, and I can see you've had a very bad fright. Nothing in the house has been moved or taken that we can see. Paul is calling the police and letting them know what has happened but probably they won't do anything since nothing was taken. That is, there's no evidence."

Tom could see his mother's analytical brain moving down the lists of options. "I suppose she'll want me to see a shrink, he thought to himself. "Maybe I should."

His mother continued. "Perhaps we've given you too much responsibility since we moved here. After all...new home, new father, new sister, new school. It must be very stressful. Sometimes when you're under a lot of stress, your mind provides avenues of escape. If anything like this happens again, we'll find a good counselor for you

18

to talk to. Our brains and emotions are very complex, Tom."

"You don't believe me, do you, Mom?" Tom whispered to his mother. "You think I'm having some sort of hallucinations or something." The hurt in Tom's voice made his mother's eyes fill up with tears.

"Oh no, Tom. I know you saw something. I just don't know what it is and I want to find out. If seeing a counselor can help us, then that's what we must do. Tom, I love you. You're more important to me than anything. Don't take offense when I try to help you," she begged.

Just then Paul walked back over to them. "Well, the police are going to keep watch for an old man with a white beard. They haven't had any reports of strangers but they'll keep a look out. In the meantime, if anything else strange happens, we're to let them know right away." He smiled at Tom.

"You're looking a bit more like yourself, Tom. Maybe we should all get away from the house for a while. Let's drive up to the cove and have a picnic before the tide turns." He looked meaningfully at Ellen.

"Sounds good to me. I couldn't do any more work today anyhow. I'll go pack lunch. Want to help, Anna?" She reached for Anna's hand but Anna ignored it and ran into the house ahead of her.

Ellen sighed and followed her stepdaughter into the house. Tom watched this exchange with anger. That little twirp! She had her nerve, treating his mother like that. Paul had watched it too and he looked back at Tom with pain in his eyes.

"It takes a while to make one family out of two," he said. "Especially when one kid keeps leaving to go to another home after the weekend."

Tom nodded and looked down at the bright golden leaves flipping across the yard. He was suddenly exhausted by everything. He wanted to go to sleep and forget all about it. But Paul reached down a large weathered hand to help Tom to his feet. He smiled and put his arm around Tom's shoulder and together they walked into the house.

The rest of the week was uneventful for Tom. School took up lots of his time and homework took up the rest. His mother made sure she was around more often so Tom was hardly ever alone in the house. He began to feel smothered and wished he could have some of his former freedom. But she was just being protective, Tom knew.

On Friday morning she seemed worried and distracted. After putting Tom's breakfast on the table in front of him, she sat down beside him with her cup of coffee. "Tom, have you seen or heard anything unusual?" she asked.

"No, Mom, have you?" he was only half teasing. She laughed with him.

"No, dear. But I have to go to Augusta today for a court case and I won't be back until after supper. And Paul is going to be away doing a boat show in Portland. You'll be here alone until I get back. Do you want me to get a sitter?"

Tom looked at her in horror. "Are you crazy, Mom? I'm twelve years old. I don't need any busy-body sitter messing around, Geeze!"

Ellen shrugged her shoulders and got up to put her cup in the sink. "O.K. Tom. You're on your own then. Anna will be at her mother's this weekend so you won't have to worry about that."

"Really, Mom. I'll be all right. I'm not afraid or anything," Tom assured his mother. Smiling, she kissed his forehead. "I kind of like you, Tom Pendly. You remind me more and more of your father." Her eyes misted briefly as they always did when she spoke of Tom's father. But her smile was just for Tom as she left for work and Tom jumped on the school bus.

She's worried, Tom thought as he rode along the bumpy road towards the middle school. Surprisingly, Tom was not. He thought about the voice that had said, "Leave him be, Pompey." It had not been a frightening voice. And who was Pompey? Tom leaned his head against the window of the bus, letting his mind run in circles. As he was getting off the bus he realized that he half hoped the old man would appear again. This time, Tom would be ready. He had a feeling about tonight and the "ghost."

School dragged slowly by and several times Tom's teachers had to remind him to stop daydreaming, or pay attention. Finally, he was on the bus headed for home. His nerves fairly tingled as he ran up the steps and let himself in the big front door.

Meet the Owner

Standing in the center of the empty kitchen, Tom's skin prickled with fear and excitement. He knew he was not alone. Slowly, he walked from room to room, looking cautiously behind doors and curtains. Even after a thorough search of the deserted house, Tom couldn't shake the feeling that someone was watching him. He made his way back to the kitchen and sat at the round oak table. Swallowing his fear, he cleared his throat and said aloud, "I'm alone now. You...you can show yourself." Tom paused and looked around. His voice echoed in the stillness of the kitchen.

For a moment there was no sound. Then, from under the table, something touched Tom's foot.

Quickly he jumped to his feet and stood shaking near the door. His breath seemed caught in his throat and his hands trembled against his sides. Nothing was there. Cautiously, he moved back to the table and forced himself to sit down.

"P...please, just show yourself. I know you're here, and I'll try to sit still."

"Woof, woof," came a muffled reply.

Quickly Tom slid back his chair and looked under the table. Only one thing said "Woof", and that certainly wasn't a ghost. There, wagging its tiny white tail, with its tongue hanging out, sat a small white poodle.

"Hey," Tom chuckled. "You're not so scary. Where did you come from, pooch?" He reached out to pat its curly head, but there wasn't anything to pat. "Oh no!" Tom groaned as he sat on the floor. "I *am* going crazy." But almost as soon as the words were out, the poodle was in front of him again. This time Tom didn't try to touch it. He just looked closely. It seemed like a real dog, except kind of misty looking. The little dog jumped up and walked into the front room. Quickly Tom scrambled after it. "Here pooch," he called.

"His name is Pompey," said a voice from the chair by the window. Tom skidded to a stop. He looked at the chair closely. "Don't stare, boy. Don't you know it's not polite?" the voice demanded.

"I...I...don't know where you are...sir," Tom said haltingly.

"Oh, sorry about that." Immediately there appeared a mountain of a man in the delicate wing chair. Although he was seated, Tom was impressed by the way he filled the chair. He appeared to be elderly, with a smooth white beard and long hair. He was dressed in a soldier's uniform, with a sword by his side. He would have been quite frightening had it not been for the white poodle seated on his lap, licking his face from time to time.

"Who are you?" Tom stammered out.

"Why, I'm Colonel Wentworth, young man, and this is my house. Now who, may I ask, are you?" The steely blue eyes focused right on Tom.

Swallowing the lump of fear in his throat, Tom croaked, "I'm Tom Pendly, sir. And I live here now...with my mother and stepfather."

"Oh, you do, do you?" demanded the old man. "Well maybe I don't want you here. Children often get in my way. What do you say about that?"

Tom was momentarily at a loss for words. He just looked blankly at the Colonel and his friendly poodle.

"Well, lad. Cat got your tongue?"

"I...I'm sorry, sir. I guess we didn't know that anybody was living in this house. We just moved to Kittery after my mother married Paul Chenard. He bought the house to fix it up. But I don't think he knew about you...sir."

"Well, not many people know about me anymore, and, as a matter of fact, I really don't care who is staying in the house. But I do have business here and I expect you to help me."

Tom was astounded. "Me? You want me to help you?"

"That seems the wisest course of action at the present time," Colonel Wentworth continued. He rose from the chair as he spoke. Pompey leaped from his lap and stood wagging his tail. Tom stepped back from the imposing figure of Colonel Wentworth.

"How do you want me to help you?" he asked.

The Colonel cleared his throat and looked a bit sheepishly at Tom.

"Well, that's the problem, lad. You see, I've misplaced something very important and I can't remember what or where. I've always been a bit forgetful and since I became a ghost the malady has gotten worse."

"The malady?"

"Yes, yes, the malady. The ailment, the sickness. What's the matter with you, boy, don't you understand English?"

Tom was completely baffled by the entire situation. He couldn't believe the way he was standing there talking with a ghost and he wasn't even scared out of his wits. He smiled a bit foolishly at the Colonel.

"I'm sorry, sir. How can I help you if you don't know what you're looking for or where you left it?"

"Oh, well, I'll remember what it is. I always remember that. I just don't have any luck finding it." The poodle had been running around the room sniffing in all the corners while this remarkable conversation had been going on. Now he was tugging at Tom's shoelaces.

"Why don't you see if your dog can find it," suggested Tom. The colonel laughed and bent down to lift the dog into his arms.

"Pompey couldn't find his way to sleep without help. But what he lacks in brains, he more than makes up for in faithfulness."

Tom watched the Colonel scratch the poodle fondly behind the ears. Pompey looked at him with adoring eyes. Rather than being afraid of Colonel Wentworth and his small dog, Tom found that he was afraid they would disappear. The colonel's brow darkened into a frown as he set the dog back down.

"You know, lad, there was a time when I knew the names of every last person in this town. I brought half of them into this world as the town's only physician. Now, I can hardly remember my own name. Why, back when I was in the war, I knew the names of all the men in our regiment, and that was over 800 men."

"Which war was that, sir?" Tom questioned hopefully.

"Which war? Why the war between the states, lad. The Civil War, of course." He looked rather contemptuously at Tom. "Children these days are rather dull characters," he observed to Pompey.

Tom blushed and studied his feet for a moment. "I never met anyone who was in the Civil War, sir. But my dad died in the Air Force."

"Oh, I'm sorry about your father, lad. We didn't have an air force during the Civil War. But we did have the use of hot air balloons. We used them for spying on the enemy."

"Wow! I never knew that! Is that your uniform?" Tom asked.

"Oh, yes. I seem to be most at home in these clothes. Strange, isn't it? I spent much more time in my physician's clothes than I did in my uniform. But, all things considered, I would rather be remembered as a soldier. "Come Pompey," he called. "We have other work to do."

Before Tom could blink, the Colonel had disappeared. "Wait, don't go!" he cried. From far away Tom heard a muffled "woof" just once...and then silence.

Walking over to the chair which had been so recently occupied by Colonel Wentworth's ghost, Tom sank into the soft cushions. His heart was thumping wildly. Had he really entertained a ghost? Would anyone believe him if he told? Should he tell his mother? That thought he discarded immediately. His mother and Paul would have him at a therapist's faster that he could think. Tom looked around the room. What could the Colonel have lost...or left here? Could something be hidden in the house? Could there be a hidden room? Lots of old houses had them.

"Wow!" He breathed out loud. The exciting possibilities in the old house were now endless and Tom could scarcely contain his excitement. Tom gazed around the room lost in this exciting dreamy state. He was brought sharply back to reality by a loud tapping on the front door.

Unexpected Help

For a moment he couldn't think what he should do. Dazed by the experience he had just had, Tom rose slowly, as if awakened from a deep sleep. He glanced out the window near the door before opening it. There on the steps stood Anna and a woman who could only be her real mother.

"Oh, no," he thought as he opened the door. "Why is she here?"

"Hello," the woman said to Tom with a nervous smile. "Is Paul here?" She looked past Tom into the empty living room. Anna just walked in and sat down on the chair nearest Tom. He glanced at her before answering her mother.

"No, Paul is at work and he won't be back until late." Tom studied Anna's mother and tried to smile politely.

"I was afraid of that," she said with a worried frown. "You must be Tom. I'm Anna's mother," she continued hurriedly. "Listen, Tom...I'm on my way to New Hampshire for the weekend and Anna doesn't feel well. I can't take her along and I'm sure Paul wouldn't mind having her for a couple of days. I feel bad about just dumping her off, but I'm in an awful hurry and I know she'll be fine with you." She pushed past Tom, who was still standing in the doorway, and kissed Anna on the head. "You go right to bed, baby, and I'm sure you'll be better in the morning."

Anna didn't look as though she felt sick, thought Tom. She just looked angry. As was he! What he didn't need was a pesky little girl in the house. They both watched as Anna's mother got in her car and drove away. Tom decided that he'd put Anna to bed right away and then he would start searching the house for hiding places. But Anna had different ideas.

"Come on, Anna," Tom said as he started up the stairs towards her bedroom. "I'll put you to bed and get you some juice to drink."

"I'm not sick and I don't want to go to bed," Anna said petulantly.

"If you're not sick," Tom replied, "why did your mother leave you here?"

"Because I told her I didn't want to go."

Tom glared at his stepsister for a moment and then shrugged his shoulders. "O.K.," he said. "Just stay out of my way then." Tom was thoroughly fed up with Anna and he didn't mind if she knew it. He felt completely frustrated by the turn of events. How could he begin his search for the missing "thing" if Anna was watching his every move?

He turned and went back into the kitchen to make a snack. Anna followed close at his heels. "Can I have something to eat, Tom?" she asked, watching as he spread peanut butter on a slice of bread.

"I suppose so," he grunted. "But don't expect me to wait on you. Get a piece of bread and I'll let you put your own jam on it."

"I don't like jam."

"So put peanut butter on it then," Tom said shoving the jar in her direction.

"I can't. It always rips the bread." Anna was beginning to whine.

"Oh, brother!" Tom exclaimed pulling the bread towards himself. "Why did you have to come here tonight anyway?!"

"I had to because my mother didn't want me along," said Anna close to tears. "Nobody wants me. I wish Daddy was home." Tom looked at Anna's sad little face and felt all the anger slipping away from him. He knew how it felt to be pushed around while grown-ups made their own plans. At least he got to live with his mother and Paul and he knew, without a doubt, that his mother loved him. It sounded like Anna didn't have that kind of relationship with her mother.

"I'm sorry, Anna," he said grudgingly. "It's not that I don't want you. It's just that I had made other plans and didn't count on you being here."

Anna walked over to the table and sat down with her head on her arms looking thoroughly dejected. Tom made her a sandwich in silence and put it on a plate in front of her. Then he poured her a glass of milk and sat down. Her eyes still had tears swimming on their rims but she was trying valiantly to hide them from Tom.

"Let's start over, Anna," Tom offered. "Pretend you just got here and I promise to be nice," Tom smiled at her and she nodded. For a moment Tom just looked at her. Then he thought recklessly, "What the heck! I might as well tell her about the ghost. What earthly harm could it do?"

"Anna...you know what I was going to do?" Anna looked at him in silence as she chewed on her sandwich. "I was going to start looking for a secret hiding place." Anna's eyes brightened and she was instantly alert.

"What kind of a hiding place?" she asked. "A hiding place for what?"

"Well," he began. "I don't know if you'll believe this or not...but...remember that ghost man that appeared last week? Well...I saw him again today...and Anna...he talked to me." Anna just stared at Tom without saying anything.

Tom hurried on. "He was here, with his dog. You'd like the dog, Anna, it was a poodle and real

35

friendly...although the Colonel said he wasn't too bright."

Anna cut in. "Who wasn't bright? Who's the Colonel? Start over, Tom. I'm all confused."

Tom felt breathless and excited again. Slowly he forced himself to explain to Anna all about the Colonel and Pompey. Anna listened raptly and asked questions until Tom felt she understood as much as he did. They had finished their sandwiches while they talked and now Tom stacked their dishes in the sink.

"So...let's get started looking for something that might lead us to the secret," Tom said, leading off towards the big living room. Anna had ideas of her own and she ran up the stairs towards her bedroom, calling back over her shoulder, "I'm going to start in my closet...there's a little door in the back of it!"

"What? Really? Wait for me!" Tom called as he thundered up the stairs after her. Anna was on her knees digging into the back of her closet when Tom raced into the room. He fell onto the floor beside her and began pushing shoes and slippers aside.

"See?" Anna exclaimed, pointing at a small square door almost hidden in the dark recesses of the closet. Tom ran his fingers around the sides of the door seeking an opening. There didn't seem to be any way to pull it. Tom tried pushing. Almost without effort, the tiny door caved in.

For a moment, the two children sat breathlessly looking into the dusty darkness behind Anna's closet. Then, slowly, Tom reached into the hiding place.

Clues

With trembling fingers, Tom searched the hole, running his fingers over the rough lathe and plaster and the musty old timbers. At first he felt nothing except the dust and webs left by generations of hidden black house spiders which live within the walls of old homes. But just as he was about to give up, he touched something cold and metallic. It fit into the palm of his hand and Tom lifted it out into the light to examine it. Anna crouched close by him as they studied what appeared to be an old key.

"What's that, Tom?" she asked. Tom gently placed it in Anna's eager fingers. She turned it over and over, then held it out for him again.

"Is it a key?" she asked. She had never seen an iron key such as this before. Tom had seen them, at least in books, but never this close.

"It's the kind of key they used to have long ago," he explained to her. "I'm not sure it's what we're looking for, but maybe when we see the Colonel again, he'll remember it."

"Will I see the Colonel, Tom?"

"I don't know, Anna, but I think he will appear again. Maybe he'll keep coming back until he finds whatever it is that he lost." Tom put the key in his pocket and together the two of them put the closet in order. "How did you find that little door, Anna?" Tom asked as they started back downstairs.

"Sometimes I sit in there and play 'family'," she answered.

"Family? What's that?" Tom asked.

"I don't know...it's like with a mother, and a father, and a brother....and everyone lives in the same house...and they all like each other. You know....like in a story..." Anna's voice trailed off as she struggled to find words for "family."

"Gosh, Anna! We have a family here. We all like each other and you're part of this family."

"No, I'm not, Tom," she said bitterly. "You're part of this family...you and your mother and my daddy. But I'm only a visitor."

This was too deep for Tom to get into. He felt like a heel for ever resenting Anna's presence in their home. No wonder Paul wanted to spend so much time with her when he had the chance. What a creep he'd been.

Tom put his hand on Anna's shoulder as they walked down the stairs together. His other hand wrapped around the iron key in his pocket and his thoughts whirled around in his head as he pictured Colonel Wentworth locking something away with that key. A gasp from Anna brought him back to the present.

A tiny white poodle bounced around at the bottom of the stairs, then raced off towards the living room. Anna and Tom exchanged excited looks and tiptoed down the rest of the stairs. Anna clung to Tom's sleeve as they followed the dog. This time Colonel Wentworth was leaning against the mantle of the old brick fireplace. His back was to them as they entered the room and Tom cleared his throat to announce their presence.

"Oh...there you are young man," he said gruffly. He pointed to the blackened bricks on the hearth.

"Many's the cold winter night I sat here watching the embers burn down, going over each battle of the war." He kicked at a loose brick. "That blasted brick never did stay in place." Finally he looked straight at Tom.

"Well, did you find it?"

"Find what, sir?"

"Whatever it is I'm looking for," he growled.

Anna shrugged and asked, "How can we find it if we don't know what we're looking for?" Colonel Wentworth smiled down at Anna. "And who, may I ask, is this lovely young lady?" Tom pushed Anna gently foreword so the Colonel could see her better.

"This is my...sister, Anna," Tom introduced her. "I told her about you and Pompey. She's going to help us find...find...what you're looking for," Tom hurried on.

"How nice." The colonel smiled. "I had a little girl once. She looked very much like you." He gazed at her fondly. "Come here, child." He sat down in a fragile antique wing chair and beckoned to her. "So, you're going to help me, are you?" Anna stood in front of the bearded ghost and nodded bravely.

Colonel Wentworth smiled at the two children and slapped his thigh. "Well, by gum! With these able-bodied helpers, I just might be able to do it this time!" He began to fade into the cushion behind him. Anna stepped back and gasped again. "Where's he going, Tom?"

"I don't know. Don't go, Colonel. We found a key!" Tom was almost shouting now. The Colonel came into focus again like a TV screen that is losing its picture.

"A key?" he thundered. "What do I want with a key? Come along, Pompey," and then he was gone.

Tom and Anna stood still in the center of the room, waiting for the Colonel to reappear. After a few moments, they moved to chairs and sat down, almost as if on cue, their legs too weak to hold them. Tom recovered first since this was his second encounter with the ghost. Anna sat quite still.

"I guess he wasn't missing a key," Tom said absently. He took the iron key from his pocket and looked at it for a moment before tossing it across the room to Anna. She looked at it on the floor, then picked it up and held it against her chest as if protecting it.

"Can I keep it, Tom?"

"I guess so." Sighing deeply, Tom got up off the chair and asked, "Do you want to look some more?"

"Where?"

"I don't know. Maybe we're going about this all wrong. If we knew more about Colonel Wentworth, maybe we could figure out what he's missing." Tom looked at Anna to see if she agreed with him. But Anna was still looking at the key and didn't seem to be paying much attention to Tom's suggestion.

He began to pace the room, not really knowing what to do next. Anna held up the key and said, "I'll bet if we could find the lock that fit this key, we'd find a clue."

"Good grief, Anna. You don't know what you're talking about. Where would we find an old lock for that key? It's probably been missing since they built this house, and whatever it went to is long gone!"

"Well, it's just as good a place to start looking as any other," Anna said stubbornly.

Tom looked at Anna thoughtfully for a minute. "You're right!" he said at last. "It is as good a spot to start looking as any other. That will be your job, Anna. You try to find anything that you think might go with that key. I am going to start looking in a different place."

"Where, Tom?"

"At the library, first thing tomorrow morning. I've got to find out more about the Civil War. And I've got to find out more about Colonel Wentworth. Since he lived right here, there's bound to be more information about him and I can start there. And I'll check on the computer for information about the Civil War. I'll be able to find out what regiments came from Maine, and especially Kittery.

Anna and Tom smiled at each other as their brains raced through interesting options.

Family Problems

Later that night when Tom's parents came home, they were surprised to find Anna tucked into bed and Tom asleep on the sofa. Gently his mother woke him.

"Tom, you can go upstairs now," she said shaking him softly. Sleepily Tom rose from the couch and moved towards the staircase. Paul touched his shoulder and asked briefly,

"How did Anna get here?"

"Huh? Anna? Oh, yeah...her mother brought her by. She said she was on her way to New Hampshire and Anna didn't feel well enough to go. But don't worry about her, Paul. She's fine. She just didn't want to go."

Paul nodded and looked meaningfully at Ellen. "We'll talk about it in the morning, Tom. But thanks for taking good care of her."

"She's no problem, Paul. She's a good kid." Tom wandered sleepily up the stairs toward his bedroom leaving Paul a bit baffled.

Saturday turned out to be a shopping day. Anna and Tom needed some school things so everyone went to the outlet stores. It was an all-day project, leaving them exhausted. Only Tom was disappointed that he hadn't had time to get to the library. There was no chance of going to the library on Sunday since the morning was taken up with Sunday school and church. Then, in the afternoon, the whole family went out in Paul's new sailboat. It was a perfect day of bright blue sky and sea, fluffy white clouds and a gentle breeze that moved them along the Atlantic shore. Anna divided her time between Paul and Tom. Tom's mother commented on it while they were taking in the sails.

"It's wonderful to see you two getting along so well, Tom. I think Anna likes having a big brother."

Anna looked at Tom and smiled a secret smile.

"Yes...it's nice." Tom added, "We found out we have a lot in common."

He winked at Anna.

"Well, whatever the reason," said Paul. "Today has been worth millions to me. I don't remember being happier." He smiled at Ellen as he rowed them from the sailboat to the wharf. Tom jumped onto the dock to hold the boat while Anna and his mother climbed out.

"Hello, Paul," said an icy voice behind him. There, waiting for them, was Anna's mother. Without pausing for a response, she swooped down on Anna like a vulture.

"How was your weekend, precious? I missed you. Look what I've got for you."

Tom felt like he was watching a movie. Anna had become rigid. Her eyes pleaded with her father to intervene. Meanwhile Anna's mother put a vibrant pink backpack into Anna's hands while herding her towards the parking lot. Anna hadn't opened her mouth yet but just before getting into her mother's car, she started to cry. "Let me kiss Daddy," she pleaded.

"Oh, hurry up then," her mother said petulantly. So far she hadn't offered any reasons why she had left Anna with Paul. But Paul had recovered his poise and he leaned into the car to kiss Anna good-bye.

"Don't cry, baby," he said softly. "Next weekend you'll be with us again." Gently he wiped the tears from Anna's face. They all watched sadly as the car carrying Anna away turned the corner and drove out of sight. The sun was still shining and the sea was beautiful, but not one of the three left standing on the dock noticed it. Paul was the first to turn away. He kicked violently at a weathered post on the corner of the dock. Tom felt like doing the same, but he moved away from his mother and Paul so they could talk privately. He remembered what Anna had said about being a visitor, and not family. It wasn't fair! Why couldn't Anna live with them? Lugging their gear up to the car, Tom's anger grew. A deep scowl replaced his earlier grin. Turning, he watched Paul and his mother walk up the path to the car. They were both silent and removed from him, and each other.

That night as Tom lay in bed he heard his mother and Paul talking.

"You're a lawyer, Ellen," Paul was arguing. "Why can't I get custody of Anna? There must be some way."

"Paul, we've been through this before. You know you would have to prove Anna's mother unfit in order to gain custody now. It would get messy for both of you and especially Anna. And it's not my field anyway. I'm a lawyer, yes, but not a divorce lawyer. If you really want to pursue this, I'll get in touch with one of my colleagues."

"You sound reluctant to get involved," Paul said testily. "I guess if it were Tom, you'd feel differently."

"Oh, Paul. You don't mean that. You're only talking from the hurt inside of you. I want Anna to live with us too. But I know what you'd have to go through to get her away from her mother."

"I'm sorry, Ellen. It's just so frustrating for me. Every time she takes her away it hurts all over again," Paul said bitterly. "I'm going for a walk!"

The house shook as Paul slammed the door on his way out. Tom lay in bed with a tight knot in his stomach. He could feel his mother hurting and he couldn't figure out how to help. Unsure of what to do, Tom sat up on the edge of the bed and looked out the bedroom window towards the harbor. The moon slid over the ocean, gently touching the sails on the boats bobbing together. Slowly he walked over to the window and knelt down, cradling his head in his folded arms on the window sill.

The houses of Kittery were snuggled into the harbor like so many kittens against the warm side of their mother, the Atlantic. Old mixed with new under cool moonlight, but if Tom half closed his eyes he could easily erase the newer buildings and picture Kittery as it must have appeared over a hundred years ago...the Kittery of Colonel Wentworth's day. His mind drifted back over the last few days, trying to sort through the pain and happiness and confusion. It was all too much for Tom. He found it easier to think about a ghostly Colonel and his friendly white dog. Lulled by these thoughts, Tom drifted off to sleep, bathed in the light of a harvest moon.

New Information

When the sun rose the next morning, Tom was already organizing his day around a trip to the public library. His mother and Paul hardly spoke at breakfast so Tom kept silent too. Just before he left for school, he asked if he could go to the library after school instead of coming directly home.

"Any special reason why?" Paul asked.

"Well, I'm trying to find out about the Civil War and about the regiments from this area."

"Really? That sounds like an interesting subject. Is it for a special project at school?"

"Yeah, sort of." Tom trailed off, embarrassed to be telling a lie but not wanting to explain. Fortunately, neither of his parents was especially interested in him since they were still immersed in their own problems. They just nodded absently.

"So, can I go to the library then?"

"I guess so," his mother answered.

The day passed slowly for Tom whose mind was busy thinking about the Civil War and not about multiplying fractions. Try as he might, Tom couldn't concentrate on school work. By the time three o'clock arrived, he had reached a fever pitch of excitement.

The public library was right across the road from Tom's house and he knew the librarians well. When he and his mother had first moved to Kittery, Tom had spent a lot of time there. He loved the smell and feel of the fine old wood and the deep quiet in the second floor rooms. The view of the harbor from the long windows was even nicer from the library than from his own bedroom. But today Tom didn't stop to look out at the ships. He knew where the historical books were kept in a special cabinet at the top of the stairs. What he didn't know was where to begin.

After looking through several histories of Kittery, Tom finally found Colonel Mark Wentworth's name. He went over the entry again and again looking for clues to the Colonel's life. Although the information was sketchy, Tom found that Colonel Wentworth had signed up with the 27th Infantry of the Maine Volunteers in 1862. They were stationed at Washington just before the battle of Gettysburg. Then there was a lot about the Medal of Honor and Tom was too confused by the information to be able to make much sense of it. The book went on to tell about Mark Wentworth being a doctor and respected businessman in Kittery. It also said he was married and had a daughter named Annie. By the time Tom had read through the book, it was nearing dinner time and he knew he should hurry home. All of the reading had been interesting, but he didn't think he'd found anything that could be a clue to what the Colonel was missing.

Supper was a quiet affair that night. Nobody seemed interested in talking and Tom felt a strange tension in the air. As soon as he could, he went upstairs to his room to do his homework. From the living room he could hear Paul and his mother talking in low tones. It worried him to hear the anger in their voices. Tom had been a baby when his own father had died. He had never heard anyone arguing with his mother. He clenched his hands in anger. No one could talk that way to *his* mother!

Behind the closed door of his room Tom paced back and forth trying to sort through it. It was all Anna's fault! If she hadn't been in their lives none of this would be happening. But even as he thought these things, he knew Anna didn't have any more control over this turn of events than he did. Suddenly, from under the bed, a small white head emerged followed quickly by a furry white body and wiggling tail. "Woof!"

"Oh, no," thought Tom. What if they heard Pompey barking? Quickly he got down on his hands and knees and called softly to the dog. "Here, Pompey."

"Woof!"

"Pompey, you be good now," Colonel Wentworth's calm voice issued an order and immediately the dog jumped up on the bed and lay quietly.

"Gosh, Colonel Wentworth. You scared me for a minute...just appearing like that."

"Oh, sorry, lad. I didn't mean to startle you. Where's little Anna today?"

Colonel Wentworth was standing in front of the window which faced the harbor. He seemed to be surveying the waterfront. Then he turned and looked at Tom with his piercing blue eyes. "Well? What's the matter, boy? Cat got your tongue again?"

"No, sir. Anna doesn't live here all the time. She lives with her mother over in Gray," Tom explained.

"What in tarnation are you talking about?" thundered the Colonel. "She is your sister, you said. Do you board her out already? She is very young to leave home."

"Ahh, no sir. My mother married her father, and Anna's mother has custody of her. We only get her on weekends and vacations."

The Colonel looked searchingly at Tom for a minute before he spoke.

"That is just about the most absurd thing I've ever heard of. You make it sound like something you trade back and forth. Why can't she just stay here?"

"Gosh, I don't have anything to say about it. The courts make that decision. I don't like it that way at all. And Anna doesn't either. None of us do, except maybe her mother."

Suddenly, from the living room, Tom's mother called to him. "Tom, are you talking to someone?" A cold sweat broke out on Tom's forehead.

"Ah, no, mom. I'm just reading out loud." Colonel Wentworth smiled at him.

"She can't see or hear me, lad. Only you and Anna can see me."

Tom was relieved at this bit of news. He continued in a whisper. "I went to the library today to find out some more about you. I thought maybe I'd find a clue to what you're missing."

"Well, you're a bright lad at that," smiled the Colonel. "Did you find anything interesting?"

"Boy, I'll say I did! But some of it I didn't understand. Maybe you could explain it to me."

"I'll try," said the Colonel, sitting on the bed with Pompey.

"There was a lot about your regiment in the war."

"Which one?"

"The 27th Infantry. Was there another one?"

"Oh yes, my boy, there most certainly was. And though I was proud of both of my units, I must say I felt greatest pride in the 32nd Maine."

"Why, sir? What was the difference?"

"Well, that's a long story, but I have the time if you've the inclination to sit still and listen." Tom sat down on the floor near the window and waited for the Colonel to continue. "You see, Lad, when I joined up with the 27th Maine, it was 1862. I was filled with the righteousness of the Northern cause. I couldn't wait to get down south to teach those Johnny Rebs a lesson. Oh yes, lad. I, who had been taught to protect and preserve life, was now anxious and willing to go end a few. But I cannot fully explain the feelings we had about the south and slavery and protecting our beloved Union. Every last man who boarded that train with me wanted to be there. We fancied ourselves as saviors, defenders of a cause mightier than ourselves. Oh, we were so full of ourselves and our cause."

Colonel Wentworth's lips trembled on these last words and he gazed off towards the sea, and beyond, to another time and place. "Well, as most soldiers find out sooner or later," he continued, "the glory of war is purchased at the price of loneliness, homesickness and boredom.

"Hours and hours of training and marching and cleaning our guns and sitting around in a dirty camp with countless other dirty men. It was not as I imagined it would be. But I stayed and did my sworn duty with the rest of my comrades.

"You see, I had wanted so badly to be there. When the war came, I was not a young man...41 years old in 1861. But, how I badgered them to give me leave to raise my own company.

"'No,'" they said. 'You're a physician,' they said. 'You're needed at home,' they said. But I knew what they meant. You're old, Mark Wentworth. Stay at home with the women and children and be useful to them."

Colonel Wentworth's voice had become hard. He scowled as if he expected Tom to argue with him. Tom sat as still as a mouse listening to the Colonel's memory, afraid to even comment for fear of breaking the spell. But the Colonel had rambled as much as he was going to. He rose to his feet and walked over to the window again.

Tom scrambled out of his way as Pompey also jumped to his feet and looked adoringly at his master.

"Hrumph," he commented to no one in particular. "The world has changed, young man, but people stay the same."

With no warning, he was gone. Pompey barked once and then he too disappeared. Tom was completely baffled by the quick change of mood and the Colonel's speedy departure. He barely had time to turn around though, when the door opened and his mother walked in. She either didn't notice Tom's momentary confusion, or chose not to comment on it.

"Hi, son. Got a minute? I really feel like having a nice, calm talk with someone," she said, "and you're elected." She smiled at Tom and he smiled back.

"Sure, Mom. I kind of miss our old talks." Tom patted the bed and his mother sank down beside him.

"I guess you've felt the tension in the house lately," she began.

"Well...yeah, I guess so." Tom was slightly embarrassed. He didn't want his mother to confide in him. He looked down at the blue quilt that covered his bed and played absently with a loose thread.

"Tom, I don't want you to worry about it. Paul and I will work everything out as well as we can. He wants Anna to live with us very much, but right now I don't see that as a possibility. The important thing is for all of us to make her feel as much at home when she is with us. I know you're doing that already, and I love you for it. You know, putting two families together isn't easy. But we're luckier than most. We really do love each other and we are willing to work at making this a complete family."

Tom nodded and reached out to hug his mother. She clung to him for a second longer than usual, then stood up and looked out the window.

"You know, Kittery looks real pretty from up here. You have a nice view of the harbor. It looks like the Kittery of long ago without all the shops hiding the water. It almost seems like I could walk out and get into a carriage to drive to the waterfront." She sighed and smiled over at Tom. She didn't see the goose bumps on

Tom's arms as he looked past her at Colonel Wentworth and Pompey.

A History Lesson

Tom sat silently on the bed after his mother left the room. Colonel Wentworth was the first to speak.

"Was that your mother, lad?"

"Yes, sir."

"She seems like an intelligent person....and a nice one. I'm somewhat tempted to make my appearance known to her too. But, adults have such a hard time with ghosts. They want rational reasons for everything, and quite frankly, they can't explain me. It makes them uncomfortable, you see."

Tom chuckled at the thought of his mother, the lawyer, trying to cope with the idea of Tom talking with a ghost. "I think you're right, sir," he said. "She would definitely have a problem with you."

"She wouldn't be the first person who had trouble with me," began the Colonel." After my daughter died, during the war, I was pretty hard to live with. I know that now. At the time, I just did the best I could. I guess I was pretty hard on a lot of my men. But," he added confidently, "we had one of the best-trained units in the Union Army. At least the 27th was well drilled and ready for action. The unfortunate thing is...the 27th didn't see much action. All that drilling and training were for naught."

Tom held his breath, hoping for some war stories that might lead him to the missing item.

"We had spent all of our time in service right outside of Washington, waiting to defend the president and the capitol. But we weren't needed at that point." Colonel Wentworth paused. "It is the irony of this life, boy, that when you think you are most prepared to do battle, you are never called upon. And then, in your weakest moment, the attack comes, and you call forth reserves you didn't know you had." He sighed, and for a moment, his huge shoulders sagged. "Ah well," he said, "If you remain vigilant, your time for bravery will come."

"What do you mean, sir?" asked Tom softly.

"What do I mean? Only this, my lad. We had waited, well prepared for battle, hoping for battle, excited by the prospect of battle...and no battle was forthcoming. Then, on the very eve of our departure from Washington to our homes back on the coast of Maine, we were called upon. The fates had timed their call upon the men for the very worst moment. Here is the situation, lad.

"It was June, 1863, and the Army of the Potomac had marched past Washington, northward, to its fateful encounter at Gettysburg. All of the soldiers around Washington had been swept along to that battlefield, leaving Washington unprotected from the enemy, so close at hand. President Lincoln and Secretary of War Stanton looked about for extra troops. The 25th and 27th Maine came to their attention.

"Now, we were about to be mustered out of the army...and many of my men were farmers who had signed on for their ninety days thinking they could be home to get the hay into their barns and the crops in from the field. They'd had their belly's full of marching and drilling and wishing they were home. They wanted nothing more of that accursed war. But, they were needed."

"So what did you do, sir?"

"I knew my duty, lad. I never doubted that I would stay. But each man had to make up his own mind, and follow his own conscience. So, on June 30th, I called my regiment out and formed it in a hollow square. Standing in the center, I read the orders of discharge and transportation home. Then I announced the president's request. I told the men that I intended to remain, and all those who would stay with me should take two steps forward on command."

"Gosh, did all the men stay with you?"

"No, lad. And looking back, my life would have been a whole lot easier if they all had. But, by actual count, 176 men stepped forward. There were arguments and fights among the men that evening over what they should do. When the transport train left that night, 550 men were on board, headed for Maine and their families. But the number who had decided to stay and protect the capitol had reached somewhere in the neighborhood of 300 stalwart men. The next day I rode into Washington and offered the services of my men and myself. Secretary of War Stanton requested the names of all those who stayed, and said they would receive the Medal of Honor."

Colonel Wentworth stopped short and looked directly at Tom. "That's it, lad," he shouted. "That's it!"

Tom leapt to his feet. "What's it?" he asked excitedly.

"That's what I'm looking for. Now don't forget it! Oh, what a relief."

Then he was gone. Again. Tom's head was spinning, trying to figure it all out. What had Colonel Wentworth meant? What had he said? The men were to be given the Medal of Honor. Is that what was missing? The Medal of Honor?

Once again Tom heard his mother calling. "Are you shouting, Tom?"

"No, yes, I mean, I'm all right, Mom. Good night!" Tom could see that when he talked to the Colonel he would have to remember to speak softly.

His mother would think he was losing his mind. Tom stood looking out the window towards Kittery. He thought again how old and peaceful it looked. Why, he could even imagine he heard a horse and wagon going by on the road below. Glancing downward, Tom blinked. There, going down the hill towards the wharfs was a genuine, sure enough, horse and wagon. Tom gripped the edge of the window sill and leaned forward. Surely the lights were playing tricks on him. He rubbed his eyes and looked again. Nothing was there...or rather nothing was on the road except a car creeping slowly down the hill.

"My imagination is running away with me," Tom said out loud to his room. There was a queasy feeling in his stomach. He stood there a moment longer and then thought of Anna. Gosh, he wished she was here now. He needed to tell someone about this, and she was the only one. Maybe he could call her. Quickly he ran down the stairs and found his mother in the living room, reading. Paul was sitting there too, working on his books for the shipyard.

"Um, Mom?"

"Yes, dear?" she answered.

"Do you suppose I could call Anna at her house?" Paul looked up at Tom with a quizzical expression on his face. Ellen looked over at him seeking his opinion.

"Sure, I guess so," Paul answered for both of them. "She'd probably be glad to hear from you. Her number's on the front of the phone book. When you're done talking, don't hang up. I'll tell her good-night." Paul smiled at Tom.

Medal of Honor

Tom's conversation with Anna the night before had been a relief. He didn't think he could have slept if he hadn't talked to somebody. And she had seemed so happy to talk to him, Tom was glad he'd thought of it. But neither of them had been able to think of any place to look for the missing medal.

Really, he didn't even know what a Medal of Honor looked like. Was it big, or could it fit in a drawer? It occurred to Tom that he'd have to do some more research. He hadn't mentioned about seeing the horse and wagon. He was pretty convinced it was just his imagination anyway.

The week passed quickly for Tom with no chance to get back over to the library. School was taking up more and more of his time. He found, to his disappointment, that 6th grade had a lot more homework than 5th. Several of the boys in his class were asking if Tom wanted to join the soccer team.

Tom wanted to join, but he was pulled in confusing directions by Colonel Wentworth. Finally, on Friday, he crossed over to the library right after school. This time he had no trouble finding exactly what he needed. There was a book on Medal of Honor winners and pictures of several different styles. He located the one that had been used during the Civil War. There was a lot about different medal recipients and each one seemed to have been braver than the last. But he didn't find anything about the 27th Maine. Maybe there was a book about that regiment. He got up to look for the librarian.

Glancing out the window, he was momentarily stunned by the scene before him. The paved road that wound between his house and the library had disappeared and a quiet country lane had taken its place. His own house was the same, yet different...more grass and flowers and big bushes around it.

A large shed or carriage house stood behind it. There were no other houses around. Further down the lane, towards the harbor, there were more houses, but no stores that Tom could see. The traffic lights were gone, the cars were gone, the 21st century was gone.

Tom's knees were shaking and he felt week. He leaned against the wall of books and took a deep breath. Hardly daring to look any further, Tom tiptoed towards the winding stairs which would lead him past the librarians and to the front door. Halfway down the staircase he leaned over the railing and looked into the center room. Things seemed a little different. Maybe the office was in the back instead of near the front door. He crouched there in the shadow for a moment, trying to decide what to do. Below him, a woman in long skirts passed through the hall to the center room. She didn't glance up the stairs. Tom rose slowly and began making his way stealthily towards the front door. He could hear quiet talking in the other rooms and a chair being pushed back from the table. Someone was coming towards him. It was too late to go back up the stairs. He stood there, uncertain which way to go, numbed by indecision.

Suddenly, below him, the tall familiar figure of Colonel Wentworth appeared. He looked up at Tom and said impatiently, "Let's go, lad. We've things to do."

1863

Tom hesitated for just a moment to adjust to the crazily tilting world around him. Then he plunged down the stairs after the Colonel.

"Colonel Wentworth," he gasped. "Where are we?"

"Look around, boy. Where does it look like?"

"But, sir," Tom gasped. "It's not the same. I mean, that's my house, or rather your house," he said pointing to the Wentworth house across the narrow lane, "but not now...I mean it looks older...or newer...I don't know, different." Tom finally gave up trying to explain it.

"That's right, lad. It's actually newer. And that is because we are now in the year 1860. The house was quite new then and not bad looking, if I do say so myself." The Colonel looked fondly at his two story home, surrounded by rolling lawns and gardens. Tom just gaped at the house, the Colonel, and everything around him. There was no logical explanation for what was happening, but then there hadn't been for talking to a ghost either. It was all quite beyond him. A horse-drawn buggy was coming up the lane from the direction of the docks. There was a large man driving, and a small white dog perched on the seat beside him. Tom looked closer and saw that it was indeed the Colonel and Pompey. He looked beside him. There was the Colonel, smiling contentedly and Pompey wagging his whole body by his stubby tail. "How can this be?" Tom asked wonderingly. "You're here, and you're there at the same time."

"Well, lad. We aren't really here at all. We are just watching, not actually participating. I thought perhaps we could find out where I left those medals if I watched myself for a while. I was a bit younger then, and not quite so absentminded. And I had the reputation for being quite reliable," the Colonel said as he watched himself jump down from the buggy and tie the horse to the granite hitching post. "I believe I was just returning from Francis Moore's home. He had been hurt in a farm accident and I had been at his house all night."

As they watched, the Colonel and Pompey walk slowly up to the front door. It was suddenly opened by a lovely young girl, of perhaps 11 or 12 years. She stood on tiptoe and kissed the Colonel, taking his black medical bag from his hands.

"Oh, Father, you look so tired. Come in and sit down. Mother just finished baking some sweet rolls and there's coffee on the stove." She linked her arm in her father's and they walked into the house together.

"That is my daughter, Anne," said the Colonel. "Not a better child anywhere. She and her mother were gentle and calm and peaceful. Not many men have been so fortunate. What a joy it was to return home from an all-night vigil at a sick bed, and find those two waiting for me. You'd have thought I was a king, the way they treated me."

The Colonel's eyes misted over and his voice cracked. "It was the saddest day in my life when I received word that Anne had died of scarlet fever. I was still with the 27th Maine, stationed in Washington, when the telegraph arrived. She was just 15 at the time. I returned home, of course. My wife was shattered; they had been so close. After the funeral I had no choice but to return to my regiment, and probably I had the easier job of it. I threw myself into the work of training my troops. More than one man complained of the drilling and marching that took place that year. But it was all that saved me from going insane. My poor wife had no such outlet. She suffered mightily."

Tom watched silently as the Colonel wiped his eyes with his handkerchief. He didn't know what to say so he just stood there silently until the Colonel composed himself.

"But, young man," continued the Colonel, "there were so many others who lost more than we did, it wasn't a time to dwell on personal losses. I remember one old woman who visited our troops near the Capitol. She was sitting quietly and talking to some of my men when I spotted them.

"'Don't be angry with them, Colonel Wentworth,' she said. 'They're just trying to make an old woman feel better. You see, today I learned that my youngest son was killed by a sniper's bullet. That makes all of them gone now. All ten of my sons, and my husband...gone. I'm alone now, but I get some comfort from talking to your men.' You can well imagine, lad, that in the face of so much heartache and sorrow, I kept my own grieving to myself."

Abruptly the old man changed the subject. "Let's take a look in the carriage house for those medals," he said, pointing to the building behind the house. Tom followed the Colonel across the narrow road and into the dark recesses of the shed. Two horses were tied in the stable which was part of the carriage house. They pawed the floor nervously as Tom and Colonel Wentworth approached. "Do they see us?" Tom asked.

"Not really," explained the Colonel. "But they sense us and that makes them nervous. The dogs really go wild when I'm around like this. Those two horses were a great pair. The big one's General, and the smaller one is Major. Yes, sir. They were quite the pair." The Colonel smiled with satisfaction. "You go look up in the loft, lad, and I'll look in the granary."

Tom started towards the stairway leading to the loft. Abruptly he turned and stared at the Colonel. "What year did you say this was, sir?"

"1860," came the reply. Tom looked puzzled. "If the war started in 1860, and you didn't receive the medals until later, would they be in the shed now?"

The Colonel looked momentarily confused. Then he smiled sheepishly at Tom as he said, "No, I don't suppose they could be. Oh, dear, you'll have to help me out, lad. I do have a way of forgetting myself. Now let's see. The battle of Gettysburg was in June of 1863. We left Washington for Maine in early July. But the medals didn't arrive in Augusta until 1865."

Colonel Wentworth scratched his white bearded chin and sat thoughtfully on a nail keg while he figured out the dates involved. Tom listened to him muse aloud while he investigated the carriage house and stable. Hanging above the stalls were all of the tack used for the horses. Tools were neatly hung on the walls or on shelves. Wooden kegs and barrels were labeled and placed against the walls, out of the way. There was a square hole in the ceiling above the horses' manger, through which hay from the loft could be pushed down. Wooden bins for grain were placed near the horses so they could be reached quickly and easily. Everything was in its place. Tom liked this building. In his own time, it was no longer standing.

"I think I have it, lad," said the Colonel. "In the winter of 1865 I got a letter from Sam Cony. He was governor then. The letter said that he had received a thundering big shipment of medals for the 27th Maine. There were 864 of them and they each had the man's name inscribed on them. Now remember, only 300 men had stayed with me in Washington so I had 564 medals too many. I asked the governor to send them to me. When I got them, I wrote down the names of all the men who had stayed in Washington with me and then I sent them their medals. I sent the rest back to Augusta. I thought that would be the end of the medal business, but I think he sent some back to me. I don't quite remember the details."

"Well, sir," said Tom, "they wouldn't be in the loft now. We'll have to go ahead a few years."

"Yes, lad, but that will have to be another day. I can stay in any century for any length of time. But mortals, such as yourself, can only stay for a short period or they can't get back into their own time."

Tom could feel a tight ball of fear in the pit of his stomach. The Colonel was so forgetful; he could easily have made a mistake about the length of time they had spent here already. Trying to control his voice, he croaked, "We'd better be going then, Colonel Wentworth."

"Right you are, lad. No time to lose."

In the blinking of an eye, Tom was once again in the library, alone, looking out the window towards the harbor. He drew a shaky breath and sat down. Things were really getting out of hand. It was enough to have a ghost visit him and talk to him. But to have that ghost whisk you back to another century was more than exciting. It was downright scary!

Mom's Surprise

Tom left the library without looking up the Medal of Honor. He was in such a daze; he didn't even remember why he had originally gone there. He looked closely at his house as he walked back across the street. The stable and carriage house were now gone, and in their place stood a garage. Where the peach and apple trees had lined the front walk, now there was scraggly grass. The lovely shady lane had turned into a busy road. Tom wondered what Colonel Wentworth thought of all the changes that had occurred since he had lived there.

Anna pulled open the front door just as Tom put his hand on the knob. The result was that Tom lost his balance and fell into the room. "Have a nice trip?" Anna asked sarcastically with a grin on her face.

"Very funny," Tom answered as he scrambled to his feet.

"And as a matter of fact, I had a very interesting trip."
He turned and walked towards the kitchen.

"What is that supposed to mean?" Anna asked. Tom
looked all around the room, making sure they were alone
before he answered her. "I just went back in time with
Colonel Wentworth. And guess where we went!"

"Where, Tom?"

"Right here!"

"Here?" Anna asked, looking around the room with
a puzzled expression on her face.

"Well, not here in this room. But here, to this house
and out in the stable and carriage house."

"The what?"

"There used to be a stable and carriage house out
where the garage is now," Tom explained. "And,
Colonel Wentworth thinks he stored the missing medals
out there."

"Well, if the carriage house is gone," began Anna,
"then where are the medals now?" Tom paused a
moment and looked at Anna. "That's the 64 million
dollar question, my dear sister. Where are the medals
now?" Just then, Tom's mother called from the kitchen.

"Hey you two! Want some veggie snacks?"

Tom made a face and called back to her. "Why can't you be like other mothers and offer us cookies and milk?"

But Anna smiled and trotted off towards the kitchen. "My mother never has time to make snacks," she said. "She lets me buy Twinkies though." Tom's mother grimaced and passed the veggies to Anna. Tom took his place across from them. The table looked festive with a fruit and vegetable platter and matching dip bowl. Juice glasses filled with Gatorade were set at each place. It was unusual for Tom's mother to be home this early on a Friday night.

"How come you get to be home so early, Mom?" he asked.

"Well, it just so happens," she began, "that I'm giving more work opportunity to my partner, which means that I'll be able to spend more time with the family, especially on weekends." She smiled at Tom and Anna. Tom paused in his eating and looked searchingly at his mother. She certainly seemed happy enough. But he knew his mother loved her work and he was surprised that she would give any of it to her partner. This must have something to do with Paul and Anna. There was a momentary twist of jealously in his belly. For them she would give up some of her work, when for the years that she and Tom had lived alone, she had steadily increased her work load.

"I thought you liked working," Tom remarked sarcastically. His mother regarded him for a moment.

"I do like my work, Tom...very much. But I think I'm feeling a bit overworked right now. I could use a bit of rest myself. I thought you'd like me to be home more often. You used to beg me to stay home."

Mother and son looked at each other. Each knew exactly what the other was thinking and their eyes held a private conversation. It was all Tom could do not to accuse her of loving Paul and Anna better than she loved him. And at the same time, he knew he was being foolish. Anna seemed oblivious to the silent undertones.

Abruptly Tom rose from the table and walked over to the sink. He steadied his shaking hand against the counter top and drew a deep breath. He really wanted to tell his mother what he'd been thinking, but he wouldn't allow himself to sound so selfish. The effort to be reasonable when his emotions were pounding made him weak. Without turning around he spoke to Anna. "Hey, squirt, do you want to go for a walk?"

"Yeah, sure." Anna pushed a carrot into her mouth and jumped up to follow Tom. His mother's voice was a bit shaky too as she said softly, "Don't go too far, you two. Your dad will be home soon."

It was on the tip of Tom's tongue to say that Paul wasn't his dad, but he clamped his lips tight and opened the kitchen door. He didn't even care that it banged shut behind them. Tom led off down towards the center of town at a fast pace. Anna trotted along beside him for a while. Then she stopped and stamped one foot. "Tom, I can't keep up with you. Walk slower!"

Automatically Tom slowed his pace to accommodate Anna. He knew he was being unreasonable about his mother and he couldn't quite figure out why he was so upset about her taking time off from work. He should be pleased about it, not angry. Anna looked up at him anxiously. "Are you mad at me, Tom?"

"No, I'm mad at my mother," he answered. Anna was astonished.

"You are? Why?"

"Well, it sounds kind of dumb I guess," Tom began. "But she never took time off from work to be with me when we lived alone. Now, all of a sudden, she can find time to stay home. But it's not for me...it's for you and Paul."

For a few minutes neither of them talked as they walked through the center of Kittery and on towards the docks. Finally, Anna ventured a comment.

"My mother doesn't stay home with me either, Tom. She says she can't afford to because I cost too much. But I think Daddy pays her some money for me so maybe she just doesn't want to." Tom was disgusted with himself and his feelings about his mother. He felt shallow and childish. And most of all, he didn't want to talk about it with Anna.

"Let's just forget it, O.K.? Maybe Paul's down here working on the boat. Race you to the dock?" Both of them took off running but Tom slowed his pace enough so that Anna outran him just as they reached the docks.

It felt good to run and the late afternoon sun warmed them in spite of the brisk ocean breeze. Paul was nowhere to be seen so Tom took Anna around the sheds and warehouses, stopping to talk to a few of the men he knew.

The sun was sinking low behind them and Tom knew they should start back towards home. Reluctantly he turned and started up the hill.

With a jerk on his arm, Anna brought him to a standstill. "What is that?" she squeaked at Tom. Tom looked up the hill towards his home in time to see a horse and wagon turning the corner. Directly behind the wagon walked a small band of soldiers in torn and grubby, blue uniforms. By now Tom wasn't too surprised when bizarre things happened to him. He looked quickly around for Colonel Wentworth, knowing he would have something to do with the changes.

"Hello again, lad," came the now familiar voice from behind them. Tom and Anna turned abruptly to see Colonel Wentworth standing on the wooden sidewalk.

Anna opened her mouth but no words came out. The Colonel chuckled at her bewilderment. Tom felt like a pro at dealing with ghosts and time changes. But he put a protective hand on Anna's shoulder realizing that she might have some trouble adjusting. She just smiled at Colonel Wentworth and waited expectantly.

"Well, Colonel," Tom began. "What year is this?"

"This is 1864, lad, and that group of bedraggled soldiers has just returned from the war. Those men are all that was left of the 32nd Maine. Of the 150 men from Maine who went into battle with me, only 22 returned to their homes. The rest were killed, wounded or missing. I'll tell you, son, in the seven months that I was with the 32nd Maine, we were in seven major battles. And we weren't the well-trained unit that the 27th Maine had been. The 32nd Maine volunteered towards the end of the war. President Lincoln had called for all the men in the country and, by gum, we had just about run out of men.

"The 32nd Maine was made up of boys, some not much older than you. Why we even had a father and son join up together. They lived through the war, but many weren't so lucky." Colonel Wentworth gazed after the tired troops who were just passing out of sight over the rim of the hill. His eyes misted with tears. "There was a troop to be proud of…every last mother's son of them."

Neither Tom nor Anna made any comment. They were trying to follow all of this without asking questions which might break up the Colonel's train of thought.

Colonel Wentworth continued. "Wilderness, Spotsylvania, Court House, North Anna, and Cold Harbor. Those battles kept us jumping for a month. One day we marched 35 miles in 27 hours, and that was in June when it was devilishly hot. But the worst was at Petersburg. General Burnside was commanding." Tom watched as Colonel Wentworth's face paled. "You'll have to see this, lad, in order to believe it." In the blinking of an eye Colonel Wentworth and the children were on the rim of a hill overlooking hundreds of earthen trenches and holes.

"Where are we, sir?" Tom gasped. He felt Anna's hand clasp his, but not a sound did she make.

"This is Petersburg, boy, and those trenches were dug by our men as permanent fortifications. We were like moles for days, digging with our knives and bayonets. Anything to protect us from the Confederate cannons and mortar." He pointed out a man who was talking to a group of soldiers. "You see that man with the long sideburns, that's General Ambrose Burnside. He was probably the most unlucky officer of the Union troops. Now watch that fort on the other side of the field."

"KA-BOOM!" The ground around them was shaken by a thunderous crash which sent the scene before them into chaos. The tremendous explosion threw a conical mountain, about half an acre in size, into the air. The fort disappeared, and with it stones, timbers, caissons and the bodies and limbs of men. Where it had stood, a gigantic crater appeared. While the dust and earth were still flying, the blue-coated soldiers began to rush into the hole. It was obvious that they were scrambling towards the Confederate troops. But the steep sides of the crater kept them trapped like so many ants in a glass jar. Confederate soldiers appeared around the rim of the crater and began to fire upon the trapped blue coats. In horror, the children and Colonel Wentworth watched the slaughter.

"It was Burnside's idea to blow up that fort and attack the confederate troops. Seemed like a bold and grand plan at the time."

As the children watched, they saw a younger version of Colonel Wentworth, bayonet in hand, leading a group of men into the crater. Over the sea of dead and wounded they pounded, rushing towards the other side. On and on they ran, firing and fighting, towards the army in gray.

Unable to pull their eyes away from the bloody carnage, the children watched in horror as the Colonel stumbled and fell, then rose again. Suddenly he spun around and toppled down into the crimson dirt. Anna stifled a scream and closed her eyes. Tom wished he could, but his eyes were riveted by the battle.

Two soldiers rushed to Colonel Wentworth's side. For a few moments they lay there, protected by the bodies of their slain comrades. They seemed to talk for a moment, then they rolled their wounded colonel onto a stretcher which was lying nearby. Bravely, the two soldiers picked up the stretcher and ran for the Union lines. Bullets, cannon balls and motor peppered the field and did not pause for the carrying party. It only took a few moments, but it seemed an eternity before the small group reached the Union trenches and passed the Colonel into waiting hands.

Colonel Wentworth sighed and faced the children again. "There were more battles in that dread war, but I had no part in them. I returned to Maine and my wife in August of 1864 to recuperate. The army doctors had patched me up pretty well, but they told me to be careful. If I ever had a bad fall, the effects of the old wound might kill me. And, you know, that's what got me in the end. I was just another casualty of the Civil War."

For a moment none of them spoke. Then the Colonel seemed to recover from his memories and focus back on the children. "You see, lad," he said looking at Tom, "I had seen the horror and the heroes of war when I was with the 32nd Maine. I knew in my heart why the Medal of Honor should be awarded, and to whom. Now, don't mistake me, I had nothing against giving the medal to those soldiers who remained with me to defend the capitol before the battle of Gettysburg. But there had to be a limit."

Tom looked at the Colonel and tried to understand where this was leading. "I'm afraid I still don't understand, sir," Tom said meekly. He was feeling rather dim-witted. The Colonel obviously felt that he had explained something and yet to Tom it was still murky. For a moment the Colonel looked mildly annoyed. But before he could begin again, Anna piped up.

"The medals only belong to really brave people, right sir?"

"Yes, child, that's just what I meant to say." Colonel Wentworth smiled at Anna.

"How many medals are missing, sir?" Tom asked in an attempt to get as many facts as possible before the Colonel disappeared again.

"Good question, lad. Now let me see if I remember all of this. There were 864 men in our company. About three hundred men stayed with me in Washington to guard the president. That leaves about five hundred and sixty medals that were sent to me to pass out which, of course, I didn't give to the men who didn't earn them. So they must be around somewhere."

Tom stared at the Colonel, open mouthed. "You want us to find 560 medals somewhere in your house?" Tom was almost yelling. This was incredible. He had expected one or two medals to be hidden. But 560! Where could the Colonel have misplaced such a vast number of medals? The Colonel just smiled and nodded. "How big are these medals anyway?" Tom finally croaked.

"Oh yes. I thought maybe you'd ask that, so I brought my own to show you." The Colonel reached into his pocket and pulled out a metallic star hanging from the talons of a bronze eagle whose wings were attached to a short red, white and blue ribbon. It was quite impressive. Both children gazed at it in awe. So this was the item they needed to be searching for. Actually, about 560 of them. Tom and Anna looked at each other and then back at the colonel. This was getting ridiculous.

"Well, children, began the Colonel. "I think I've given you a lot to think about for one day. It's best we get back to your own time."

In the blinking of an eye, Tom and Anna found themselves on the busy street in Kittery which led to their home.

"Where are the horses and the soldiers?" breathed Anna, looking all around. Her little face was pale in the fading afternoon light.

"I honestly don't know," replied Tom as he reached for her hand. "I guess they're back in their own time. But I wonder where Colonel Wentworth stays. He travels back and forth in time so often; he never seems to be at peace."

Tom looked off towards the harbor, lost in thought. "I wonder if that's why he needs to find those medals. Maybe he can't be at peace until he does. I've heard about ghosts wandering about in time because they had unfinished business to take care of. Maybe that's why the Colonel came to us." He looked at Anna to see if she agreed.

"You mean that we have to find those medals or the Colonel won't be able to go to heaven?" Anna asked.

"Something like that," Tom said. "Anna, we better not tell the folks about Colonel Wentworth or this time travel stuff. At least not for a while. I think we have a better chance of helping the Colonel find those medals alone. I mean, if you told your dad what had just happened to us, he'd probably think we were making it all up anyway. So let's keep it a secret for a while longer, O.K.?"

Anna nodded her head at Tom but her face was a pitiful mass of confusion. "I don't like keeping secrets, Tom. I always tell when I'm not supposed to. But I'll try."

Tom smiled at her and took her hand. "That's all I ask of you, squirt. I know how hard it is to keep a secret from your dad and my mom. But for a while at least, let's both try."

Salty mist from the harbor settled around the children as they trudged up the hill towards home. Tom had completely forgotten his anger at his mother and he smiled at her when they walked into the warm kitchen. The aroma of freshly baked bread greeted them and Anna ran quickly over to the side board to peek at the golden loaves resting there. Tom looked at his mother.

"I didn't know you could make bread."

"Well, my dear son," she teased him. "There's a lot of things you don't know about me. For instance, I love to bake and now that I'm going to have more time off, I'm going to do just that!"

Tom smiled at her sheepishly. "Well, you won't have any arguments from me about that."

"Can we have some bread?" Anna piped up.

"You bet. Just as soon as the table is set for supper and your hands are washed." Tom turned to follow Anna out of the kitchen but his mother gently touched his arm.

"Are you still angry with me, Tom?"

"No, Mom. I was just being stupid. I'm glad you're going to be home more." Again Tom turned to go. But just as he was leaving the room, his mother asked him one more question.

"Tom, have you seen any more of that ghost? You haven't said anything about it and I didn't want to bring it to your mind if you had forgotten it."

Instantly Tom's mouth went dry. "Ah, no Mom. I haven't seen a thing." He kept his back to his mother and continued to walk out of the kitchen. She couldn't see his cheeks and neck flaming red. Keeping this a secret was going to be harder than he or Anna had suspected. His heart was pounding as he ran up the stairs to join Anna and he didn't see his mother standing in the middle of the kitchen with her hands on her hips, and a worried expression on her face.

Building a Family

Saturday morning dawned with the crisp brilliance of October in Maine. Everyone was in a festive mood at breakfast and Paul proposed a trip up to the Moosehead Lake region to view the fall foliage. They packed a lunch and headed north, driving through the farmlands and wooded hills of central Maine. Tom hadn't had a chance to see this area so he was intensely interested. As they passed through Augusta they saw a sign which said, "Camp Keyes." It was also the airport sign so Tom asked Paul where the camp was. "Oh, there's not a lot there now, Tom. But it was where the old troops in the Civil War came to train and practice before they went south."

Tom looked at the flat-topped hill and wondered if Colonel Wentworth had been here. At the words "Civil War" Anna had picked up her head and looked at Tom. But she didn't say anything and the moment passed. Tom smiled at her and winked. The day passed quickly and that terrific feeling of being a complete family enveloped them all. Anna had started to call Tom's mother "Mom" so Tom jokingly called Paul "Dad." He was surprised when Paul smiled at him and said, "That sounds nice, Son."

Sunday was church day and Anna and Tom went to Sunday school. Some of Tom's friends from school went to the same church and they always sat together afterwards while waiting for the grown-ups to visit. Anna shyly hung around Tom until one of his friends asked who she was. Tom smiled at her and said, "Oh, she's my sister." It had been on his mind to say stepsister, but he realized that he really thought of her as his little sister.

All too soon the weekend had passed and Tom and Anna hadn't been alone for a minute. Just before Anna was to leave for her home, Tom pulled her aside and whispered, "Look, Anna. I'm going to have to search for those medals without you. Where do you think I should look?" He didn't really think she'd have a suggestion but he wanted to include her anyway. He was surprised when she whispered back to him.

"I've been thinking about it, Tom, and I think they might be buried somewhere." Tom scratched his head and thought about it a moment.

"You may be right, Anna, but I can't go around digging up the whole yard looking for them. We have to find some more clues, and I don't have any idea where to even look for them."

"You need to talk to the Colonel again. Ask him if he had a secret hiding place for his gold and stuff."

Tom almost laughed out loud. "What gold, Anna?"

"Well, maybe not gold, but things he liked a lot...you know what I mean." She looked impatiently at him.

"O.K.," he agreed. "I'll see what he has to say about that."

Paul called from the driveway. "Hurry up, Anna. I promised to have you back at your mother's by five o'clock." Anna and Tom walked quickly towards the car where Paul was waiting.

"Bye, Tom," Anna said softly.

"See you next week, squirt," Tom patted Anna's head and winked at her. Long after Anna and Paul had driven away, Tom stood in the driveway looking down the road. It was really strange how much he liked having a little sister. A year ago he never would have thought he wanted anybody to live with him except his mother. When she had met Paul, Tom had welcomed the male companionship. He had enjoyed going to the docks with him and learning to sail. Anna had seldom been a part of their days together. It wasn't until after the wedding that Tom had really understood that Anna was going to live with them, at least part of the time. Then he resented her intrusion into the family that Paul and Tom and his mother had so swiftly created. As Tom gazed thoughtfully down the winding road, he realized that he hadn't really begun to accept Anna until Colonel Wentworth had appeared.

Almost as soon as the thought crossed his brain, the Colonel appeared beside him. As usual, Tom was momentarily jolted by the sudden appearance of the tall, stately figure, accompanied by Pompey. Quickly he glanced around to see if anyone else was watching.

"Remember, my boy," said the Colonel as he observed Tom's glance, "Nobody else sees me but you and the girl."

"Right!" agreed Tom. "But somehow I never quite believe that."

The Colonel chuckled. "I understand. But now we must get back to business. It has occurred to me that you need some help. And since I don't seem to remember where those medals have been placed, I thought perhaps you might find something in my diaries. They were always kept locked up in a special box which I hid behind the walls of my daughter's bedroom. I can't be sure of course, but they might still be there."

Immediately Tom thought of the key that he and Anna found in the wall behind the closet of her room. But there hadn't been any box. At least he didn't think there had been.

"We did find a key back there, sir," Tom began. "Remember, we told you about it? But I don't think there was any box there."

"Which room did you find it in?" asked the Colonel.

"The one with the small window which faces the library."

"Well, no wonder. That room was for my Tom...Tom Murray. He was a young, colored boy who showed up one day in our camp when I was with the 32nd Maine. The poor little fellow was no bigger than a pepper-box and he didn't seem to have any family anywhere. He attached himself to me during the war, and when I came home, I didn't have the heart to leave him behind.

"He lived here with us for the rest of my life. Worked for the Boston and Maine Railroad when he was a man. Good worker, Tom was. And a good friend. At any rate, that was his room in the front of the house. My daughter's room was the room you stay in now."

"Where in the wall did you hide the box, sir"? Tom asked quickly. He was going over every inch of the room in his mind. Where could the Colonel have hidden a box there?

"If you look just beneath the window facing the harbor," began Colonel Wentworth, "you will see a small piece of the wall which looks as though it was patched.

Push on the left side of the patch and slide it at the same time. That's where I always hid the diaries."

Almost as soon as the words were out of his mouth, the Colonel disappeared and Tom took off running for his room.

The Diaries

As Tom tore up the stairs towards his room, his mother appeared in the kitchen door and called after him, "Tom where are you going in such a hurry? Do you have any homework?"

"Ah, yes, Mom, and I haven't started it yet. I have to hurry now."

"O.K, Tom. You shouldn't leave it till the last minute like this. When you're hungry, you can make yourself a sandwich. Do you need any help?" she asked, almost as an afterthought.

"Gee, no, Mom. It's only math and some reading in science. I just need to get at it."

His mother walked back into the kitchen shaking her head and mumbling something about checking on his homework more often. Tom watched her disappear and then he scrambled into his room and shut the door. Sure enough, there below the window was a small place in the plaster that looked patched.

Could it be possible that after all these years, Colonel Wentworth's diaries could still be in there? With shaking hands, he pressed the left side of the patch and tried to slide it at the same time. At first nothing moved. Tom tried it again and pushed harder this time. The door had evidently weakened from years of disuse and the slightest pressure now made the wall crumble beneath his hands and a small black hole appeared.

Trembling with excitement, Tom reached into the empty space. Sure enough, he felt a package beneath his fingers. Carefully he lifted it out into the light. At first glance it looked like old newspaper. Then he realized that the newspaper was actually wrapped around a book. Painstakingly he unwrapped the newspaper, making every effort not to rip it. There, in his hands, lay not one, but three small leather-bound books. Tom could hardly breathe as he opened the first of the books. The date on the top of the first entry was 1862. It began:

Today we left Kittery for Boston on the first leg of our journey into battle. The men are all in fine spirits and anxious to put down this insurrection. Most of us feel this will be a short war, since the south is ill prepared to do battle against our superior forces. Already it has dragged on longer than Old Abe predicted. The train moves swiftly. Tomorrow we should be in Washington.

This was like stepping into Colonel Wentworth's brain, thought Tom as he quickly read the next few entries. He looked at the dates on the top of the pages and realized that he needed to look in the other books. Taking the third book, he quickly checked the date.

June 1864, Had a laugh today. The Minister came for dinner and we had all bowed our heads for grace when Polly, that brazen parrot, said, "Do ya want yer head scratched?" Mother didn't think it was funny, but the minister had a chuckle.

September 1865, Today my old hip wound pained me something fierce. I put salve on it and that helped somewhat. I wouldn't mind the pain of the wound so much if it didn't conjure up memories of the battle when it happened. Every time the wound throbs, I see again poor James Chase lying next to me in that damned crater. His face covered with blood and his one eye hanging on his cheek. How that boy lived is beyond me.

Tom could see that crater all over again and the broken, bleeding men scattered around it. He read on.

October 3, 1864, Today received letter from James Chase. He has returned to the war after he received a glass eye to replace the one lost in the Battle of the Crater. I marvel at his valor and bravery.

Tom skipped ahead a few entries. He needed to find something about the Medals of Honor.

January 1865, Today received surprising letter from Governor Sam Cony. Says he received all of the Medals of Honor which should be handed out to the 27th Maine. Wanted to know what it was all about and what should be done. I answered him immediately asking him to send me all the medals assuring him that I would take care of them. Odd thing about those medals...there was precious little done to earn them. I must be careful not to allow them to be delivered into the hands of the undeserving.

Again Tom flipped through the entries. *March 1865, Today have sent out all of the Medals of Honor to those men who remained with me in Washington to defend the president during the Battle of Gettysburg. There were 560 extra medals which I will not distribute. I'll send them back to Washington and hope that this is the end of the medal business. Knowing how the red tape of bureaucracy wraps around the easiest of tasks, it won't surprise me if they show up here again. And if they do, I'll simply hide them where nobody will ever find them.*

Hurriedly Tom skipped ahead looking for a clue as to where that hiding place might be.

April 1865, Wonderful news today. The war is ended! My wound is only one small reminder of the battles I participated in. The deeper scars, I know, will never heal. But I thank God that at last the fighting is done. The Union is secure. The slaves are free. The United States is again United.

Tom read that entry several times. He was beginning to have an understanding of the Civil War. It was so much more than dates and battles. Freeing the slaves had been only a part of the reasons for those four bloody years. Keeping the United States whole had sent Colonel Wentworth to battle. And it had been reason enough for brave men to lose their lives.

Tom gazed out the window towards the Kittery harbor. He imagined himself marching off to battle with the soldiers dressed in blue. Shaking himself free of his thoughts he turned again to the small book in his lap. Tom read the last entry to see how long the Colonel had kept this diary.

December 1865, Mother and I decorated the house for Christmas today. It was a sad affair without Anne to help out. I believe that the war has changed us all and a sadness surrounds our nation which was not there before. I look to the year 1866 to begin the healing which now must come. I can tell one thing...I'm perfectly content to stay right here in Kittery for the rest of my life.

Tom held the book quietly for a few minutes, just staring off towards the harbor. He really felt as though he knew the Colonel now. But he didn't know any more about where the medals were hidden than he did before. Tom tried to sort out all the information he had. He knew that there used to be a stable and perhaps the medals had been hidden in there. So where would they have been moved when the stable was torn down? Or perhaps they were buried, in which case Tom had a monumental task ahead of him. Or they could be hidden in something which was locked with the key they had found in Annie's room. Where would the Colonel have hidden them so nobody else would find them?

Notes of Interest

Tom spent the rest of the night reading over all the diary entries, from 1862 to 1866. Everything fascinated him but nothing led him to the hiding place of the Medals of Honor. He didn't want his parents to find out about the diaries just yet. He wanted to share them with Anna first.

The sun was just lighting the eastern sky when Tom hid the diaries in the wall and pushed a chair in front of the hole. His eyes were scratchy with lack of sleep and he fell exhausted across his bed. Sleep claimed him immediately and two hours later his mother knocked on the door to wake him for school.

Tom was so tired that he actually felt sick to his stomach. Groggily he made his way downstairs and sat at the breakfast table. His mother looked alarmed when she saw him. "What's the matter, Tom? Are you sick?"

"Ah, yeah...I guess so. My stomach hurts. I just want to lie down," he said weakly.

"You look awful. You march right back upstairs and go to bed." She rested her cool hand on his forehead momentarily. "You don't feel hot. I guess I won't call the doctor until after lunch. Maybe by then you'll be feeling better."

Tom didn't argue with her. The only thing he wanted was his pillow. Gratefully he made his way upstairs again and flopped down on the bed. Within minutes he was asleep.

Tom groaned when he looked at the clock on his dresser. Twelve o'clock! The entire morning had vanished in waves of dreams about soldiers marching wearily through bloody battlefields. All of the soldiers had fallen, and all of them were wearing the Medal of Honor. Rubbing his eyes, Tom pushed back his covers and climbed out of bed. He stood at his window looking at the harbor which was being drenched in a cold autumn rain. It looked about as bleak as he felt. He was standing there when his mother knocked softly at the door before entering with a neat lunch tray.

"Feeling better, Tom?" she asked as she set the tray on his bedside table.

"Yeah, lots better." Tom answered truthfully. He looked at the food hungrily. "Thanks Mom. I'm hungry enough to eat two of everything." Tom's mother laughed softly as she sat in the chair Tom had placed in front of the window. He glanced nervously down at the opening in his wall which hid the precious diaries. "You know, Tom," began his mother. "You've been acting rather strange lately. Is there anything you want to talk to me about? So much has been happening in our lives this last year, sometimes I miss the calm of our lives before Paul and Anna. But I am happy and I hope you are too."

"Yeah, I'm happy, Mom. And yes, I like Paul and Anna." His mother smiled at him, catching the teasing tone in his voice. Tom wished fiercely that he could tell his mother about Colonel Wentworth and the medals. In some ways it would make his life so much easier. On the other hand, she would never believe him and that would cause even bigger problems. So he gave her an explanation she could handle.

"You know, Mom. It's not easy starting in a new school. You have to start at the bottom of the pecking order. And school is harder this year too."

"Is there anything I can do to make it easier for you, Tom?"

Tom sighed. "I guess not, Mom. Some things you have to do on your own. And this is one of them."

"Well, are there any boys from school you'd like to have over? Maybe Paul would take you and some friends on a sail. You could go out to the island for lunch."

Tom brightened at the thought of a day on the sailboat with Paul and a couple of guys from school. There were a number of guys that would jump at the chance to do that.

"That would be great, Mom."

"Well," she said as she picked up the lunch tray. "I'm glad we had this little talk. What are you going to do with the rest of the day?"

"I've still got homework to finish Mom, and some reading to do." As soon as his mother left the room, Tom pulled the diaries out of the hole in the wall. He lined them up in his desk in order of the dates and took out his note pad. Somewhere in these diaries, he reasoned, there must be a clue as to where the Colonel would hide something valuable. For the rest of the afternoon, Tom took notes of anything which seemed a clue.

At three o'clock he read back over the notes he had taken:

1. Sam Cony sent the Colonel the medals in a large box. But each medal had its own box and they were about six inches long.

2. Some of the medals were sent to the proper owners. Others were not.

3. Tom, the black boy who had come home from the war with the Colonel, had lived in the room where Anna slept. He was fiercely protective of the Colonel.

4. The carriage house was used as a store room too. It was torn down and a garage was built on the site.

5. The house has remained basically the same since the Colonel lived in it.

6. The only new structures the Colonel mentioned building on his property were a front porch, in 1865, shortly after he returned. And a flag pole, which he only mentioned the intent to put up, but never actually said he

completed. He did say that he needed to get cement for the base of it. Tom looked at the pitiful facts he had come up with. No mention of a key or strongbox. No mention of the medals at all except to say he had received them. He was more confused than ever. His head actually pounded from the forced concentration of the afternoon. Running his hand through his hair, Tom pushed his chair back and looked out the window. Everything seemed to be spinning around in his head. Where could he look that he hadn't already looked? The attic was sort of off limits because the floor was only half boarded over. He might be able to sneak up there some time when Paul and his mother were both gone. There was also a basement which was more like a dark, dank hole. Tom had been down there when Paul was investigating the rafters. Sighing deeply, Tom gathered up the diaries again. Wrapping them carefully in a paper bag, he put them back into the wall. Then he pushed the chair back in front of the hole. He knew he'd have to tell his mother about the diaries soon enough. But for now he needed to keep everything quiet. Luckily Tom was expected to keep his own room clean, and as long as he did that, his mother wouldn't come snooping around.

The smell of supper cooking brought Tom to his feet. He needed to stretch his cramped legs and arms. Running down the stairs, Tom called out to his mother that he'd be outside getting some air.

"Don't go far, Tom. Supper is almost done," she called back.

Tom breathed deeply of the crisp autumn evening. The leaves were almost all down from the oak and maple trees. They made a thick brown carpet in the back yard. Tom kicked through them as he strolled around. Leaning against the garage, he wished that it was a stable with horses in it.

"Woof, woof!" Tom looked around for Pompey and the Colonel. Sure enough they were walking towards him, blowing the leaves into little whirlwinds with each step. Tom smiled at them. "Hello, Colonel. I found your diaries and read through them. They sure are fascinating."

"Yes, I rather thought you'd enjoy them. Did they help you find the medals?"

"No. But I do have some more questions that might help." Tom sat down and leaned against the garage. The Colonel sat near him looking perfectly at home. Pompey lay on the leaves by Tom's feet. He tugged at Tom's shoe laces.

"Why can Pompey touch me, sir, but I can't touch him?"

"Strange about that, Tom. Animals seem to go through this time travel in a different dimension than humans. He certainly likes you. Perhaps that's why."

Tom reached over to pat the dog, but Pompey simply wasn't there. His hands ached to touch the little white ball of fluff.

"Go ahead, lad," the Colonel prompted gently. "Perhaps your questions will jog my memory."

"Oh yes. Well, sir. You built a porch on the house after you returned from the war. Could you have hidden the medals in the framework?"

"Hmmm. Now let me see. I didn't actually do the building on the porch. I had some men do it for me. I was very busy with my medical practice. Kittery was growing by leaps and bounds then."

"O.K. You ordered some cement for a flag pole to be put up. Would you have buried the medals in the cement?"

"I don't think so, lad. But that would have been a good place."

"O.K. Could you have hidden them in the attic or the basement?"

"Well, here's the thing, lad. I don't think I hid them any place except the carriage house. But they were moved after I died and I don't know as I ever knew who moved them. It could have been Tom. Or it could have been a very good friend of mine, Charles Farwell. Charles did a lot of work for me after the war. He knew all about the medals and how I felt about them, as did Tom. Either of them could have taken the medals or hidden them on his property."

Tom looked aghast at Colonel Wentworth. "You can't expect me to find them if they've been removed from the property, Colonel."

"Right you are, lad," the Colonel nodded thoughtfully. "But you see, I can't rest until I know for sure and certain that the medals will never get into the hands of undeserving men. They mean too much to me. I saw the men who died and suffered in the War Between the States. I know who earned the right to that medal. And I know that there are those who would claim them without that right." The colonel sighed and looked with sorrowful eyes at Tom. "Keep looking, lad. It's all I can ask of you."

With that he disappeared. Tom sat still a moment. Two truths hit him at once. One was that Colonel Wentworth was not going to leave until he found those medals. The other was that it was probable that Tom might never be able to find them. Up until that moment, he had never thought of that possibility. It had all seemed like a good and exciting game. Now he realized he was in over his head. He was going to need some adult help and he didn't think his mother was the person to ask. That left only Paul. Would he believe Tom? Would he help? There was only one way to find out.

Help

The tension in the house had been somewhat relieved when Tom's mother had decided to spend more time at home. Suppers were smoother affairs and they all found more to talk about. But tonight Tom was unusually quiet. He kept thinking about what Paul was going to say about Colonel Wentworth. He cleaned off the table without being asked and then sat on the foot of the stairs while Paul and his mother finished their coffee. As soon as Paul started towards the living room, Tom approached him.

"Paul, ah I mean, Dad...could I see you for a few minutes? There's something I want to ask you."

"Sure, Son." Paul smiled at Tom. "What's up?"

"Ah...I think we'd better go to my room. I have to show you something."

Paul followed Tom up the stairs with a slight frown on his sun-browned face. Once inside the room, he closed the door and faced his stepson.

"O.K., Tom. Now what's this all about?"

"You'd better sit down. This will take a while," cautioned Tom. Heaving a sigh, Paul sat on the edge of Tom's bed and Tom pulled the chair away from the window to expose the hole in the wall.

"What the..." exclaimed Paul.

"Now wait a minute before you say anything, Paul. This is very complicated so I'd appreciate it if you didn't say anything until I'm done. Then you can ask all the questions you want." It took Tom the better part of an hour to explain all that had happened to himself and Anna since they had met Colonel Wentworth. Paul had gone from tolerant to skeptical to angry to mystified. His questions were very precise, first making sure that Anna had not been in any danger. He looked at the diaries with fascination and held them reverently. When at last Tom came to the end of his story, Paul sat silently staring into space. At last he looked at Tom and said, "You know this is impossible. Ghosts don't exist." Tom didn't say anything. He just looked at Paul and waited some more.

"O.K., Tom. Suppose Colonel Wentworth does exist. What can we do? You say he won't leave until the medals are found. You don't suppose we would be the first people to look for those medals do you?"

"I don't know. Do other people know about them?" Tom asked.

"Well, there's ways to find out about that. We can call the state house in Augusta and inquire into this medal business. And we can ask around town if anybody knows anything. Old Jake Farwell still lives down by the docks. He might be related to the Farwells that Colonel Wentworth spoke about. I'll ask him tomorrow."

Tom felt a great burden being lifted from his shoulders. He looked gratefully at Paul and smiled. Paul had believed him and was going to help him. But what about his mother? What would she say?

Long after Tom had gone to bed, he lay staring into space. Suppose Colonel Wentworth got mad because he'd told Paul. Suppose, even with Paul's help, they weren't able to find the medals. Would Colonel

Wentworth be here forever? That would be awkward for the whole family, but Tom would miss the old man and his dog if they never came again. It was becoming more involved and confusing every day. Tom drifted off to sleep at last. He didn't know that a tiny white dog lay curled at his feet and Colonel Wentworth stood at the foot of the bed looking off towards the harbor and beyond.

The next day when Tom came home from school, Paul was sitting at the kitchen table sipping a cup of coffee. Ellen sat across from him, making idle drawings on a napkin. They both looked up when Tom entered.

"Hi!"

"Hi, yourself," answered his mother.

Paul pushed a chair in Tom's direction and smiled at him. "I told your mother everything, Tom. Now you tell her too. She has questions." Tom and his mother locked eyes in silent conversation. Hers were worried and skeptical. His were guarded. Tom sat down.

"Tom," his mother began." This whole thing is so bizarre; I don't know what to think. Start at the beginning and tell me everything you can remember. I'm going to take notes. It may help all of us." So Tom went through the story once again. He was glad to tell his mother at last. Keeping secrets from her was the hardest thing he'd ever had to do. Paul went through two more cups of coffee before Tom finished.

When Tom stopped, Paul spoke at last. "This is what I did today, Tom. I called the state house and the museum in Augusta. They were very helpful and told me almost the same story your Colonel Wentworth told you. The medals were sent back and forth from Mark Wentworth to Sam Cony, the governor, a couple of times.

Eventually Wentworth kept them all and that was the end of the whole mess officially. The lady at the museum said that they'd be worth quite a bit if they were found." Ellen was watching her son while Paul was talking. Two little worry lines appeared between her eyes. She frowned but kept silent.

"Gee, Paul, does that mean you'll help me look for the medals?"

"Don't see what harm that could do," answered Paul. He shrugged his shoulders apologetically at Ellen.

"You don't believe this fantasy about a ghost, do you Paul?" she asked.

"Well, I don't rightly know what to believe, Ellen. Tom had the story right and he didn't change it a bit from the first time he told me."

"Well, I don't think we should encourage him in looking for things that don't exist."

Tom listened to this exchange with anxiety and growing anger. He looked hard at his mother and said, "You may not believe me, Mom, but everything I told you is the truth!"

"Oh, Tom. It's not that I don't believe you. It's just that I don't believe in ghosts. Your truthfulness is not in question at all. But I'm afraid I'd need more solid evidence before I launched into a search for missing Civil War medals."

"Did you show her the diaries, Dad?"

"Yes," Paul answered. "And we both think they should be turned over to the state archives or something. Those are some precious."

"Well, Mom. If you saw them, you know that Colonel Wentworth told me where to find them. How would I ever have found them myself?"

"That is a good question, Tom. How did you find them yourself?"

"Oh, Mom. I already told you. Anyway, you can ask Anna. She saw the Colonel too."

"I don't think we'll talk to Anna about this until the weekend," said Paul. "If her mother got wind of this, we'd never get to have her, even on weekends." He looked pointedly at Ellen. Tom sat quietly for a moment. Then he pushed back from the table.

"I have homework to do. If you want to help me look for the medals, I'd appreciate your help. But if you don't believe me, I'll just keep looking by myself."

He left his mother and Paul sitting silently at the table. Almost as soon as he shut the door to his bedroom he heard a familiar "Woof" and Pompey ran out from under the bed.

"Hey, Pompey. Where's your master?"

"Right here, lad," came the familiar reply. "I see you've called in the big guns." Tom looked at the

Colonel, searching for signs of anger. But the clear blue eyes looked steadily back at him and Tom nodded his head.

"Yes sir. I told my stepfather and he told my mother. But I needed their help, Colonel Wentworth. And you do too. I just don't see how I could find those medals by myself, or with Anna's help."

"Right you are, son. You did the right thing. But it remains to be seen how they accept all of this. They may not be as much help as hindrance, you know. Be that as it may, the deed is done. We now must use them to our advantage." Tom sighed heavily and sat on the edge of his bed.

"How do we do that, sir?"

"Well, your stepfather seems like a man we can trust. He is willing to help with the search. Perhaps we need to make my personage known to him. What do you think, lad?"

"You mean you'll appear to Paul?" Tom jumped off the bed. "I'll call him up here right now." Tom could hardly believe this good news. He didn't want to give the Colonel any time to change his mind. Opening the door,

Tom called down the stairs. "Paul, will you come up here for a minute? There's something I need to show you." Tom couldn't keep the excitement out of his voice. Paul's head appeared around the corner at the bottom of the stairs. He took one look at Tom's face, then bounded quickly upward.

"What's up now, Tom?"

"Just come here quick, Dad." Paul strode purposely into the room but stopped immediately when he saw the tall distinguished gentleman leaning against the wall.

"Woof!" Paul looked startled but he stayed firmly in the room. Tom looked from Paul to Colonel Wentworth. They both seemed to be waiting for the other to speak. Finally, Tom took over. "Um...Paul, this is Colonel Wentworth. Colonel Wentworth, this is my stepfather, Paul Chenard."

Colonel Wentworth was the first to speak. "How do you do, sir?"

"My pleasure," responded Paul automatically. He reached out to shake hands with the Colonel, but then took his hand back when he realized that there wasn't any hand to shake. Colonel Wentworth smiled at Paul's momentary embarrassment.

"I realize how difficult this must be for you, Mr. Chenard."

"Please, call me Paul."

"Thank you," continued the Colonel. "Meeting a ghost is not an everyday occurrence and I appreciate your forbearance in this matter. Your son, here, has been most patient and helpful thus far."

Paul looked at Tom and smiled.

"He's a good boy," he agreed.

"The problem," began the Colonel, "is that finding the medals may be beyond the boy's ability now. If I knew they were in the house, then perhaps he could find them. But they may be buried somewhere on the property and for that he will need your permission and assistance." Paul nodded thoughtfully.

"I want to help you out, sir, but frankly, I don't know where to begin. Have you got any idea where we should look?"

"Quite frankly, I don't. To my best recollection, they were in the carriage house when I died. My feeling is that they may have been moved to a safe place by either of my friends, Tom or Charles Farwell. Now whether they moved them to their homes, or hid them here, I don't know."

"Well," began Paul, "I'm willing to help out, as I said before. But we may not be successful. What will you do then?"

"Just as I've done ever since I died. Try to find them myself or find a mortal who can help me. I have been haunting this house for the last 100 years. And I will continue to do that until the medals are found and disposed of."

Paul ran his hand over his face. "Right. Well, Tom and I will do our best, Colonel Wentworth. That, I can promise you."

The Colonel smiled and looked at Tom with his blue eyes misty. "I've never asked more than that from any man. I thank you."

And with that he was gone. Pompey barked and wagged his tail, then he was gone too.

Paul moved to the bed and sat down shakily. He looked at Tom and shook his head. "Whew, that was a first for me, Tom. I've never even thought of talking to a ghost before. And he is...was...quite an imposing ghost at that. Holy Toledo! And this isn't the type of thing you run out and tell anybody either. If I told the guys at the dock that I'd talked to a ghost, they'd laugh me off the wharf. And your mother will not want to hear this. Boy, oh boy...I can see what you've been up against, Tom."

"Well, first things first. We need to make a plan of attack. Tell me anything you think might be of help."

Tom grinned at Paul's reaction to this predicament. He was taking the bull by the horns and taming it. Tom got up to grab his notebook from the desk.

"I took these notes from the Colonel's diaries," said Tom. "I thought maybe they could lead me to a clue." He handed the book to Paul.

"Say, this is very good, Tom. Your mind sort of works like your mother's. Lay everything out in neat solid lines to see if you can make any sense of them. Very nice." He read through the notes several times.

"Hmmm. I'd like to start in the attic first. I've never really looked up there too well. But I can certainly tell if there's an area that doesn't fit with the lines of the house...a place for hiding things. Let's go, Tom."

The two of them headed for the attic stairs when Ellen called from the kitchen, "Hey you two. Where are you going?"

Paul stopped and looked at Tom before calling back down the stairs. "Oh, Tom thought there might be mice in the attic, Ellen. We're going to look for signs up there."

Tom raised his eyebrows at Paul. They grinned at each other and continued up the stairs. One light in the attic illuminated the slanted roof above their heads and not much else. The dark corners stayed hidden. Paul turned to Tom and said, "Go fetch my flashlight from the kitchen, and maybe you better bring up a mouse trap too. You know, to make it look legitimate."

Tom took off at a run down the stairs. He was having fun again. The full weight of the responsibility was lifted from his shoulders. Now Paul was in charge and Tom could enjoy the search. He skidded to a stop in the kitchen and asked his mother where the flashlight was. She pointed to it and continued to wash the dishes in the sink. She didn't seem to be curious at all. Great! No need to lie.

As he ran back up the stairs with the flashlight, He didn't see his mother put down the dishtowel and tiptoe after him. Nor did they hear her softly enter the attic after they busied themselves looking in the darkest corner. So it was a complete surprise to both of them when they emerged from the dust and cobwebs a half hour later to find her sitting on a box watching them.

"Find anything interesting, gents?" she asked sarcastically. "Like mice...or medals?"

Paul was the first to recover. "How long have you been watching us, Ellen?"

"Long enough to know that you're looking for those medals. Mice indeed! You could have at least trusted me enough to tell me what you're up to."

Tom's mother sounded hurt. Paul and Tom exchanged sheepish glances.

"Gosh, Mom. We really didn't think you'd approve of us looking for the medals. We weren't trying to hurt your feelings." Tom moved over to sit down beside her.

"I may not completely believe in your ghost, Tom. But I believe in both of you," Ellen said looking from one to the other. "I don't want to be left out of something so important in your lives."

Paul pulled her to her feet and put his arms around her. "I'm sorry, Ellen. I keep forgetting that you're one person I can trust. If I forget it sometimes, it's because I've had some bad experiences with trust in the past. But I'm working on it. Just don't give up on me, O.K.?"

"You know I won't, Paul. This family is going to make it. We'll all have to work on it. Now, let's see what you found, besides mice."

They showed Ellen several old bottles and an antique hammer, but no medals or hiding places. Brushing the cobwebs off their clothes, they started back downstairs. Paul put his arm around Ellen's shoulder and winked at Tom. "Looks like we have another helper for our search, Tom. I think tomorrow we'll try the cellar." Tom looked at Paul gratefully and touched his arm.

"Hey, Paul...I mean Dad. I really appreciate this, you know. I didn't know where to turn next. Thanks."

"Well, you know, Tom, it's kind of a challenge. Fun too. I'm glad to help, Son. Now you get on to bed."

Later, as Tom drifted off to sleep he could hear his mother asking all about the cellar and the Colonel. He smiled...this was another load off his mind.

The Search Is On

As Tom was stuffing his backpack the next morning for school, Paul walked into the kitchen.

"I'm going up to Augusta today to read the official records about the medals, Tom. We may not have time tonight to go dig up the cellar. As a matter of fact, we'd better wait until Saturday. We'll have the whole day to search, and in the meantime, maybe I can find out more information about this business. By the way, how often does Colonel Wentworth appear to you?"

"Well, it's different. Sometimes he appears twice in one day, and then I might not see him for a week. He seems to kind of know when I'm working on the case. Then he comes around and helps me out."

"So...probably you won't see him until Saturday, right?"

"Yeah, I guess so. But it's hard to say."

"O.K. If you happen to see him, tell him I'm enjoying this." Paul chuckled. "I think your mother is beginning to like it too. Although she says she positively doesn't want to see the ghost."

The week passed quickly for the whole family. Tom was busy making up for lost time in school. His mother worked full time for the rest of the week. Paul was hardly around at all. Tom did ask him if he'd learned anything in Augusta.

"Not much more than was in the diaries. I asked where people donated historical documents though, so that I can turn them over to the right people when the time comes. For the time being, I'd just as soon nobody knew about those diaries. I think probably the newspaper will make a big deal over them and we don't need that for a while."

Anna arrived on Friday night and Tom explained all that had happened since she'd left the week before. Her eyes were bright with excitement as she thought of seeing the Colonel and Pompey again. But when Saturday arrived, Anna's mother appeared too. She didn't even get out of her car so Paul had to go out to talk to her. When he came back in he was seething.

"What's the matter, Paul?" asked Ellen.

"That witch!" he exclaimed. "Now she says that Anna can only stay here once a month. After this weekend she's to stay with her except for the third weekend of the month."

"She can't do that, Paul," Ellen protested. "You have visiting rights weekly."

"She says that Anna is difficult to control after she's been with us, and she will take it back to court if need be."

"We'll just see about that! I'll call Ed Hartly. He's the best divorce lawyer in the state. He'll find out about this!"

Ellen marched off to the phone. Anna watched Ellen leave the room, then she looked at her father.

"Can Mommy do that, Daddy?"

"No, Anna. I won't let her!" Paul sat near Anna on the couch and put his arms around her. He spoke more calmly. "I won't let her take you from me if I can do anything at all to prevent it. We'll take it back to court.

She won't get you." Tom stood rooted to the spot by the door. He didn't know what to think. The day which had seemed so sunny only moments before now appeared dark and gloomy.

Slowly, in a daze, he wandered from the room and out the front door. He walked out to the road and looked back at the house. It looked calm enough on the outside, but Tom knew it was seething with unrest on the inside.

Hands in pockets, Tom headed for the harbor. Suddenly there was a tiny white dog trotting along beside him. Startled, he looked up to find the Colonel walking next to him.

"You seem a bit down, lad. Care to tell me what is wrong?"

"Oh, Colonel Wentworth," began Tom. "It's my stepsister, Anna. You see, her mother doesn't want her to stay with us except for two days a month. And Anna wants to live with us so we can be a real family, and we want her too." Tom explained all he could about Anna's custody problems and her feelings about family to the Colonel, who asked questions whenever Tom paused.

"And I don't know what to do to help." Tom's voice trailed off into silence. For a moment Colonel Wentworth didn't say anything. Then he looked thoughtfully at Tom.

"Perhaps there's something I can do...I am a ghost remember. And there can be advantages to this state." Tom studied the Colonel who was rubbing his hand over his beard.

"Hmmm...I'll have to give this some thought, lad. In the meantime, I seem to recall that today was the day we were going to look for the medals."

"Oh, gosh, Colonel. I clean forgot. Maybe searching for the medals will take Anna's mind off this custody stuff." Tom sighed. They turned around and headed back towards the house.

Immediately the Colonel disappeared. Pompey, however, trotted blissfully along beside Tom. "Gee, Pompey, I wish you were mine. We'd have fun together." The little dog frisked around Tom's heels for a moment longer, then, cocking his head to one side as if hearing a command, he yipped once and was gone.

When Tom got back to the house, he found Anna and her father beside the bulkhead which was the only entrance to the basement. The stairs leading into the darkness below were a combination of dirt and rocks. Paul was studying them as Tom approached.

"Are you ready to look for the medals, Tom?"

"You bet! Is Mom going to help?" Tom looked at Anna's flushed face. He could see that she'd been crying but she smiled at him now. She held out an extra flashlight to Tom.

"No, she said she'd keep an eye out for intruders." Gratefully Tom took the flashlight and they began their cautious descent into the cool dampness below his house. At first, even with the narrow beams of their flashlights, they couldn't see very well. But gradually their eyes adjusted as old rafters and posts led off into the darkness beyond them. Paul had to stoop over but Tom and Anna could stand upright.

"I'm not sure exactly what we should be looking for, kids." Paul looked around him. "You two head off towards the front of the house, I'll take the back. I suppose anything that looks strange or different will be something we should investigate."

Even though Tom couldn't see the Colonel, he felt his presence. As they moved off together, he whispered to Anna. "I think Colonel Wentworth is with us right now. Maybe we'll get lucky."

But forty minutes later, they were still pawing through dirty rafters, beams, cobwebs and rocks, when he felt a tug on his sleeve. Anna had moved off to the back of the house to be with Paul so Tom was startled.

"Wha?"

"Tom, I think that is the chest over there," an excited voice spoke in Tom's ear. Tom looked over his shoulder but nobody was there.

"Colonel Wentworth?"

"Oh, sorry, lad." Immediately the Colonel appeared beside him. His normally neat uniform was covered with dust and dirt and there were cobwebs in his white beard. "Look over there by the ledge."

Tom looked where the Colonel was pointing. There was a corner of the house that was held by a granite ledge. Tom couldn't see anything sticking out. "Where, Colonel?"

The Colonel bent over next to the ledge and rubbed at the dirt. Nothing happened. "Oh, bother! I can't move this dirt. You come here, lad."

Immediately Tom was on his knees beside the Colonel rubbing away at the granite. But to Tom's surprise it wasn't granite at all. It was wood and it was a box.

Discovery

After Tom's frantic cries, Paul and Anna had arrived in seconds to investigate and then lift the heavy wooden crate from the corner of the house. In the end they had to get ropes and a "come-along" to help pull it out and then up the stairs into the sunlight. They all held their breath as Paul chiseled away at the ancient lock which dangled from the front.

"Wait!" cried Anna. She pulled a necklace out from the front of her shirt and there was the key which they had found more than a month before. Paul took the key from Anna and placed it in the lock. Slick as a whistle the old lock gave way and Paul put his hand on the lid.

"Don't open the lid, sir." Colonel Wentworth's commanding voice startled all of them. They swung around to find him standing there in his war uniform, sword by his side. Pompey lay on the ground at his feet.

"Why shouldn't we open the lid? Isn't that why we searched for these medals?" Paul demanded.

"You have done me a great favor, my good man," began the Colonel. "But I must ask that you not look at the contents of the box or you won't be able to finish the task we have started."

"You'll have to be clearer than that, Colonel Wentworth," said Paul. He stood with his hand on the lid of the box but made no move to open it. The children looked at the Colonel and then at Paul.

"Yes, of course. You see, Mr. Chenard," began the Colonel patiently. "Those medals are made of gold. They have the names of many men on them who fought beside me when I was with the 27th Maine. They were good men, and loyal soldiers. However, they did not earn the right to those medals, nor did their heirs. If you were to look at them, you would be tempted beyond human endurance to either sell them or give them to a museum or send them to the families of the deceased soldier whose name is on the medal. It is imperative that those medals be disposed of forever in a way that they can never be found again."

Colonel Wentworth looked straight at Paul. For a moment neither of them spoke. Then Paul sat heavily down on the lid of the chest. "What did you have in mind, Colonel?"

Colonel Wentworth smiled at Paul. "You are a very intelligent man, sir. You also have the assistance of two fine young people. I will leave the matter of disposal to you and them. When the chest is gone, then I shall also be gone...and I will not have to return here again. I will be free to remain with my loved ones in the hereafter."

In the twinkling of an eye, the Colonel and Pompey had disappeared. Tom looked at Paul and Anna. They stood motionless, as if held in a spell. Then Paul got up off the chest and said, "Give me the key again, Anna." Swiftly, he locked the ancient lock once more. Tom and Anna looked at the chest and then at Paul.

"What'll we do, Dad?" Tom asked.

"I'll pull the truck up here and we'll take the chest down to the boat. Run in and tell your mother about this. See if she wants to go for a sail." Paul headed towards the garage to get the truck.

Anna and Tom closed the bulkhead door and then Tom ran in to tell his mother what had happened.

"Tom," she said nervously. "This whole thing gives me the willies. If it's all right with you three, I'll stay here and hold down the fort. You be careful." She kissed Tom quickly and watched him run out of the kitchen. There was a faint smile on her lips but worry in her eyes.

Tom and Anna helped Paul load the trunk into the back of the pickup. They covered it with a tarp and tied it down.

An hour later found them moving slowly out into the channel away from Kittery and civilization. Tom sat on the trunk watching the coastline move past. He thought about the medals which were hidden in the chest and had a terrible longing to see them. How could they be sure that the medals were all inside if they didn't look?

Anna was sitting beside Paul in the stern and he was letting her hold the tiller. They wouldn't notice if he just peeked inside. The thought had hardly taken root when he heard a cheerful yipping near his feet. Looking down he saw Pompey sitting beside him. Colonel Wentworth did not make an appearance. It was the first time since

Tom had begun seeing them that Pompey appeared alone. It seemed strange and exciting. But the urge to open the chest passed and Tom was content to watch the shoreline.

Paul called to Tom over the whipping of the sails in the wind. "We'll head for the outer islands and throw the chest out there. That way we'll know where it is if ever we need to locate them for any reason."

Tom nodded that he'd heard him but the wind had come up and was whipping Paul's words away. The small white caps on the waves had given way to deep swells. The sky, which had been blue and clear just moments before, was now filling with racing clouds. Paul watched with concern on his weather-beaten face. Anna pulled the hood of her sweatshirt over her head and slid to the bottom of the boat. Tom moved back beside her.

"Where'd this come from?" Paul muttered to the children. "We'll have to hole up at the cove on Emmet's Island. Probably this'll pass before too long."

Tom had been to Emmet's Island for a summer picnic with Paul and Ellen. He remembered it as having a snug friendly cove where they'd put down the anchor for an afternoon of swimming. As they approached it now, the snug harbor had turned into a frothing, bubbling mass of waves.

"I'm going to put out the sea anchor. Tom, you reef the sails. Anna, you lie down!"

Tom could hardly hear Paul over the roaring of the wind. He put his arm around Anna and felt her shivering through her thin jacket. All of them were soaked from the splashing spray. Tom was surprised to see Pompey sitting right near the chest in the front of the boat. He didn't seem to be frightened at all.

"Watch out!" screamed Anna. Bearing down on them was a surging swell. Their boat sank into an inky black trough and before it could rise onto the next crest, the wave smashed into them. Tom couldn't remember what happened next. He closed his eyes and held onto Anna as the water closed over his head.

Safe

When Tom next opened his eyes, he was lying in a puddle of sea water in the bottom of the boat. A slow gentle rocking soothed him as he raised his head to look about. Anna was lying beside him and Paul was working on something in the bow of the boat. Paul noticed Tom sitting up and nodded to him. "What happened?" Tom asked shakily and he pushed himself to his feet. Paul shook his head.

"I wish I knew," he said. "I never, in all my years of sailing, saw a squall come up so fast, or leave so quickly. The mast broke when the wave hit and I got clunked on the head. I don't remember anything after that." He rubbed his head and grimaced.

Tom looked around him. The boat was rocking gently in the cove and the sky above them was calm and blue. The mast was indeed broken, and part was lying in the water. Other than that, everything looked the same.

Everything, that is, except that the trunk was gone and Pompey was gone too. "Where's the trunk, Paul?"

"Somewhere in the ocean, Tom. I guess the Colonel wanted to be sure we didn't know where exactly those medals were dropped. All I know for sure is that they're gone."

"Where are we?" Anna asked weakly as she sat up brushing her hair from her eyes. Paul immediately moved to the back of the boat to sit beside her.

"Are you all right, Princess?"

"I guess so. I thought we were all going to be killed though."

"Yeah, I guess we all did. But, seems like we're O.K. except for the broken mast. I cut the stays and the mast off. I think we can rig something up and limp home. The motor still works."

Paul reached behind him to adjust it. In a moment they all heard the reassuring throbbing of the motor as it churned to life. Tom and Anna watched the island disappear as they chugged along over the now calm sea towards Kittery and home. The sun was dipping into the ocean as they tied up to their mooring.

They remained thoughtful and quiet as they drove back home in the pickup. As soon as they pulled into the yard, Ellen came running out of the house.

Before they could begin to explain to her why they'd been late, she pulled open the driver's side door and hugged Paul. "You'll never guess the good news! Anna's going to stay with us."

Memories

The three of them had tumbled out of the truck and followed the excited Ellen into the house as she told them a fantastic tale. Shortly after Anna's mother had been at their house that very morning, she was in a car accident. She wasn't seriously hurt, Ellen quickly reassured everyone, but she told the police such a crazy story, they took her to the hospital for evaluation. They thought she had a concussion.

"What story?" asked Paul

"You'll never believe it, Paul. She told the police that a ghost was riding in the car with her. He was dressed in a Civil War uniform and had a little white dog on his lap. And he had talked to her. She was hysterical, of course. The police had a terrible time calming her down. The doctors think she should have a complete evaluation before they make their decision. But in the meantime, Anna gets to stay with us.

"Now, it's only temporary, but I talked to the judge who handled your custody case, and he thinks it very likely that you'll be granted at least temporary custody of Anna. And we can ask for a reevaluation anytime."

Paul grabbed Ellen and hugged her tight. "You just gave me the best news of my life." He turned to Anna and whirled her around the room. Tom stood by the table with a foolish grin on his face.

When Paul put Anna down at last, she ran over to hug Tom. Then she turned to Ellen and held out her arms.

"Oh, Anna," Ellen sighed as she pulled her into a tight embrace.

"I couldn't be happier." Ellen looked at Tom over Anna's head and smiled. "Can you believe that story, about a ghost? Imagine that!" Tom grinned at his mother and Paul and Anna. Then he laughed outright.

"Who would think up a ghost story like that?" Soon they were all laughing and crying and hugging again. Paul and Anna began to tell Ellen about their fantastic day. Tom listened for a minute but then he had an urge to go up to his bedroom. Slipping quietly upstairs, he went in his room and shut the door. First Tom looked at the empty hole in his wall, and then above it to the view of Kittery out his window. It seemed as empty as he felt. What was it Colonel Wentworth had said? "As soon as you dispose of the medals, I will be gone too."

Tom sat on his bed and let his thoughts drift back over the last month. It was truly unbelievable. His entire life had revolved around the Colonel and the "medals of honor." And somehow that had all been interwoven with their struggle to keep Anna. Tom shook his head and lay back against the pillows. How was he supposed to go back to living a normal life now? He closed his eyes and gave in to the overwhelming fatigue he felt. In his dreams he chased a poodle through the ocean trying to put a medal around his tiny white neck.

The next day Tom and Anna surprised Paul and Ellen by making breakfast. They laughed at the slightly burned hotcakes and weak coffee, reveling in the euphoria which had enveloped the house. It seemed they couldn't get enough of each other. They all talked at once and laughed at nothing in particular. Tom smiled so much his face hurt. Right at the top of the list of things to talk about was enrolling Anna in her new school the next morning. Anna was so excited she could hardly stay in her chair. She would be at a different school than Tom so he couldn't help out much. But the excitement was infectious and the day passed in easy pleasure.

The only thing that marred it for Tom was the fact that nobody seemed willing to talk about Colonel Wentworth. Once he had brought up the fact that he would miss the Colonel now that he was gone. There had been an uneasy silence for a moment and then his mother had changed the subject.

After two more attempts to talk about him to the adults, he had finally gotten Anna alone and asked her if she missed the Colonel.

Anna looked uncomfortable and then she admitted that she was having trouble remembering him. "I don't mean to forget him, Tom. But somehow I just can't think what he looked like at all. I just don't like to talk about him, that's all."

Tom was bewildered. What was happening to them? Why were they forgetting about the Colonel? Were they deliberately trying to ignore what had happened?

Anna started school and by the end of the first week she had made new friends. Tom had a friend, Jerry, come over the next weekend. He was funny and smart and Tom really liked being with him.

Paul fixed the hole in Tom's wall and the diaries were given to the historical society. There had even been a piece in the paper about how Tom had found them in his room. But the excitement died down quickly and everything returned to normal.

Life went on. Anna's mother was getting therapy at Augusta and she didn't seem in any hurry to try to get Anna back. Paul and Ellen had filed for complete custody and it looked as though they were going to get it.

So why was Tom so moody? He didn't understand it himself. He should be happy. But something seemed to be missing from his life. At night when he went to bed, he expected to hear the "woof" of a tiny poodle or the booming voice of a mighty Colonel. He had only known them for a few short weeks. Why did he miss them so much now? Why wouldn't anyone admit they had existed?

There seemed to be a weight on him that did not affect the others. He walked through his days slightly bewildered. His dreams were full of Civil War battles. Around every corner he looked for the Colonel. Each time he looked out his window he expected to see the Kittery of the 1860s.

For the first time since it had all started, Tom felt like he was losing his mind. His mother worried about him. Paul said it was just teenage growing pains which he would get over. Anna was immersed in new friends and new school activities.

One day, just before Thanksgiving, Tom walked over to the library after school. He leafed through the book from which he'd found out about Colonel Wentworth's life. Gazing out the window towards the ocean, Tom thought back to the day he and the Colonel had visited the 1860s. What a fantastic journey! A smile touched his mouth and tears misted his eyes. Quickly he brushed them away. Sighing, he closed the book softly and looked around him. Somehow, he felt the colonel was closer to him here.

"Now you get out of here you silly little puppy." Tom could hear the librarian downstairs scolding a dog. Immediately he sat up and listened.

"Here, here, get out from under those tables. Shoo!"

Tom got up slowly and put back the book he was reading. He walked to the staircase and leaned over so he could see the hallway below. There, looking directly up at him was a tiny white poodle.

"Pompey!" he breathed. Then louder "Pompey!" He stumbled down the stairs to where the poodle was dancing around avoiding the librarian's fly swatter.

"Is he your dog, Tom?" she asked. "You know dogs aren't allowed in the library. Please take him home."

Tom knelt down on the floor and the puppy bounded up into his arms. Joyously he licked Tom's face. The librarian laughed. "I can see he's yours all right. What a cute puppy." Tom nodded at her and stood up with the dog still in his arms.

"What's his name, Tom?" She reached over to scratch the fluffy white head. Without hesitating, Tom answered, "Pompey."

"That's a funny name for a dog. Where'd you get it from?"

"Um...I got it from a good friend...I got the dog from him, too."

"Well, you've got a friend right in your arms, Tom." She held the door open for him. Only after he had crossed the road with the puppy licking his face and wriggling all over, did Tom stop to investigate him more closely. He had a collar and dog tag. Tom held it up so he could read it better.

"My name is Pompey II. I belong to Tom Pendly." On the back was the symbol of the Medal of Honor. Tom studied it a moment. Then he slipped the dog tag off the puppy's soft neck and put it in his pocket.

"They don't want to believe in the Colonel or you, Pompey. So you'll just be a little lost puppy who needs a home. Maybe someday I'll show them your dog tag. For now, it's enough that the Colonel sent you back to me."

Just then the door burst open and Anna ran towards them. "Tom, where did you get the puppy?" she cried delightedly. Kneeling down beside them, she tried stroking the furry white body, but the puppy was too busy jumping and rushing in circles to sit still for it. Tom watched Anna to see if she would recognize the dog. Apart from her pleasure in the puppy, there was no sign that she knew him. Sighing, Tom reached in his pocket for the dog tag.

"What will you call him, Tom? Can you keep him?" Anna laughed as the puppy ran in circles around them.

"His name is Pompey, and yes, I think I can keep him. A...a friend gave him to me."

"Oh, you're so lucky. Can I help take care of him?"

"Sure, Anna. I think you'd be a big help taking care of Pompey. And you're right...I am lucky. Now, let's go in and show the folks."

Anna ran ahead to open the door and Tom picked up Pompey. He hugged the tiny wriggling body close to his face and whispered, "Thanks, Colonel." Then he and Anna walked in to show the family their newest addition.

* * * * * *

Mark F. Wentworth, Brevet Brigadier General, U.S.V., served as colonel of the 27th Maine and the 32nd Maine during the Civil War. His home was in Kittery, Maine, and all the facts given about his life are as true as this author can detect. Even his dog, Pompey, really existed. The Medals of Honor were indeed given to the 27th Maine for exactly the reasons stated in this story. Colonel Wentworth awarded the ones which were earned, and then he hid the rest. The mystery of the whereabouts of those medals has never been solved. Most of the factual information in this book came from *A Shower of Stars* by John J. Pullen.

About the Author

Barbara Winslow, author of three children's books, taught school in South Dakota, the Alaskan bush, and Maine. A school teacher for 36 years, Mrs. Winslow loves history and storytelling. Her three children patiently listened to many stories growing up, and now pass them on to their own children. She continues to live in Norridgewock with her husband in a house built in 1876.

CPSIA information can be obtained at www.ICGtesting.com
Printed in the USA
BVOW08s0339170516

448355BV00001B/1/P